Rockin' Summer

SAMANTHA MICHAELS

Thank you to my husband and my dog for putting up with all my craziness.
Thank you to my friends for all the support.
Thank you Zoe for being the best PA and now proofreader an author could want!
There a lot of people in the book world I would like to thank, but need to call out a few very special people by name: Lala, JJ, LouLou & Maryann! Love you gals!
Finally, and most importantly, the readers who've supported me: THANK YOU!!

Chapter One

Lexi

"**A**re you finally ready?" Damien yells from the living room.

If I don't get my ass moving, he's going to leave my home. I can't believe it's only been a couple months since Dave knocked me down, the best thing that's ever happened to me. Now, tonight, I get to show up at my high school reunion on the arm of my sexy man. Not only that, but my former classmates are in for quite the surprise. The introverted bookworm they all knew and hated was gone. I put the finishing touches on my makeup and newly dyed chestnut brown hair, and walk downstairs, where I'm greeted by a whistle.

"Holy fuck, you look so damn hot, woman."

"Thank you. I gotta tell you, I love the scruff you're sporting. Not to mention how good it feels when, well, you know!"

I feel the heat creeping up my cheeks. I should be used to Damien's compliments by now, but I still find it hard to accept. He couldn't be more different from Bryan. I shudder just thinking about him, grateful he wasn't in our class. Damien and I walk outside just as Judd is walking

1

over. He agreed to join us tonight, so Melissa didn't feel like a third wheel. We head over to pick her up on our way to Yoder's Banquet Hall. Damien has his Sirius XM Radio turned to Octane.

"It's time for Test Drive." the DJ says. "First up tonight, we have the debut single from up-and-coming singer, Lexi Carter." My mouth drops open. How the hell did my song end up on Octane?

I look over at Damien. "Did you know about this?"

"No clue. Must have been Xander."

I think back to that phone call from Dean.

"Hey Lexi, Xander listened to your recording and asked me to share his feedback."

"Okay, let me have it."

"He was blown away. Said he hadn't heard talent like that in a long time."

"Are you serious?"

"Damn right. He gave me a song that he wants you to record."

Other than Damien, nobody knew about it, but they sure do now. I didn't know he was planning to give it exposure like this. Maybe that was better, as I wouldn't have agreed to it. I hate to admit it, but it's kinda cool hearing it, especially on one of my favorite music channels.

"Girl, holy shit. I love it," Melissa said.

"Amazing song," Judd said.

"Thanks." I'm trying not to cry.

We pull up to the banquet hall, walk into the lobby and head to the registration table. The woman sitting there's name tag reads "Jessica." I remember her being one of the bimbo cheerleaders that used to make fun of me. Her face has a lot of wrinkles and she has plenty of gray hairs, which makes me smile more than it should.

"May I have your name, please?" Jessica said.

"Alexis Carter."

Jessica's eyes went wide. "Are you sure?"

I look over at Damien and flash him a look.

"I hope so or I have the wrong name tattooed on my dick."

I didn't even bother trying to control my laughter.

"This is my boyfriend, Damien St. James."

Jessica writes our names on two blank tags and hands them to us

2

without a word. We waited outside of the ballroom for Melissa and Judd. The room has a dance floor in the middle. Tables surrounded the floor on three sides and the food and bar area on the fourth side. A DJ has a booth in the corner, playing music popular in the year that we graduated. The colors of the linens matched our school colors, blue and gray. Melissa and Judd joined us, and the four of us walked in together. I saw quite a few heads turn when they saw us. Might be the tight jeans and low-cut black t-shirt I'm wearing.

"Babe, they're all looking at you," Damien whispered in my ear.

"Let's give them a show."

We walk to the dance floor. 'I'm Too Sexy' by Right Said Fred blasts from the DJ's speakers. Damien and I dance. His hands are on my hips as I shake my ass. Melissa and Judd join us and she matches my moves. The song ends, so we go find a table. I see Doug with his wife Meg, so Damien and I sit with them while Melissa talks to some of her former teammates.

"Nice little show, girl," Doug said. "I hope they're all eating their hearts out at what they missed."

"Thanks, Doug. I was always lucky to have you as a friend," I said.

After Melissa and Judd join us, we check out our old classmates. Just like when I saw Jessica, I couldn't help but smile when I saw people who used to make fun of me for not looking so good. I'm a nice person, but the way some of these people treated me back in high school, I'm allowed to feel smug.

"Let's go make the rounds and see how the rest of our old classmates look," Doug said.

"I'm in," Melissa said.

Doug always understood me in a way Melissa couldn't. He was like the male version of me, a quiet, studious type. We spent a lot of time together studying or reading. He was overweight throughout school, but after graduation, he joined a gym and got himself in shape. I smiled when I saw all the jaw drops from our female classmates when they saw him.

"Look at all these bitches drooling over you, sexy beast," I said.

"You're having the same effect on all the dickheads, girl," Doug said. "We may not have been king and queen of the prom, but I'm declaring us king and queen of this fucking reunion." Doug and I pretended to crown each other and returned to our table arm-in-arm.

"Dare I ask?" Damien said.

"Doug and I named ourselves king and queen of the reunion."

The rest of the table laughed. I see Jessica walk into the room and over to a bunch of women. They all turn and look at Damien, their faces looking like someone just farted. I laugh out loud, remembering her face when Damien made his naughty comment.

"What's so funny?" Doug asks.

I fill him and Meg in on what Damien said at the registration table and they burst out in laughter. I look over at my sexy man, and for the millionth time since we met, I smile thinking about how he came into my life. As we were sitting there, the DJ played (Everything I Do) I Do it For You by Bryan Adams.

"Babe, let's dance."

"Love to."

Damien leads me to the dance floor and pulls me tight against him. We sway together to the music, still getting nasty looks from Jessica and her friends. I whisper in his ear about our audience. He lowers his head and kisses me hard. He slides his tongue into my mouth and sets my body on fire. We might need to visit the coat room later!

After the song ends, the DJ announces that the food is ready, so we walk back to our table. Melissa, Meg and I get in the food line while the men grab drinks. After we eat, we're sitting at the table chatting.

"As bad as high school was for me, I'm having a blast tonight," I say.

I see the doors to the ballroom open, and all the color drains from my face. What the fuck is he doing here?

Chapter Two

Damien

I hear Lexi gasp. I look over and all the color has drained from her face.

Melissa follows Lexi's gaze and says, "Fucker."

I don't need to ask Lexi who that is. It takes every ounce of my self-control not to kick the shit out of him. You're not that guy anymore, I tell myself. I haven't told Lexi everything about my past and, for now, I want to keep it that way. I'm not sure she'd understand why I was that way, especially after the way she'd been treated by her classmates.

"I can't believe that bitch Amy brought him here," Doug said.

I see Amy and Bryan approaching our table, but before they get a chance to say anything to Lexi, Doug and Melissa stand in front of her, hands clenched into fists at their sides. I've never seen a more smug look than the one on Amy's face.

"Well, well, it's the reject table," Amy said.

"Fuck you, bitch," Melissa said.

"Still classy, I see."

"What do you want?"

"To show the pig that Bryan has a real woman now."

"Too bad you don't have a real man. Hope you have a magnifying glass when you're in bed."

"Fuck off, bitch," Bryan snarls.

"Whatever, tiny," Melissa said.

"What's wrong, Lexi? Too afraid to say anything? Damn good thing you couldn't have children. I'd hate to think what they'd be like," Amy said to Lexi.

I was about to ask them to leave when I felt Lexi leave my side. I watched her pull her arm back and let it fly, knocking Amy on her ass. I stood there in shock, as did the rest of our table. Jessica came running over and helped Amy up.

"Satisfied?" Bryan said to Lexi.

"Not yet."

"Haven't you done enough to Amy?"

"What about what you did to me? All the times you told me I was fat and ugly. All the times you ordered me around and threatened to hurt me if I didn't comply. Or that sex ended when you were finished, with no regard to my needs. I let you steal my self-esteem to the point that I stayed and took everything you handed me. Bad news, dickhead, that girl is gone. You're the biggest asshole I've ever known. Despite that, I'm still grateful for our time together. Had it not been for you, I wouldn't know what a real man was like. Unlike you, Prince Limp Dick, Damien has no problem satisfying me. Have fun fucking the cheerleader after this."

Lexi puts her hands on Bryan's shoulders and connects her knee with his groin. Hard. He doubles over, his breathing labored.

"Now I'm satisfied, fucker."

She walks back over to me and leans against me. I wrap her in my arms as Bryan attempts to walk. I've never been prouder of her than I am right now. I'm also extremely turned on, and all I can think about is getting her home.

"You okay, babe?"

"I've never been better. That was long overdue. I'm sorry, though, that you guys had to see that."

"Don't be," Doug said. "You're a badass."

"You never told me any of that," Melissa said, tears in her eyes.

"I couldn't bring myself to tell anyone. It hurt too much."

I watch Melissa hug Lexi. She hadn't told me that level of detail either. I hated hearing what Bryan put her through, hearing the pain in her voice. I hope this brought her the closure she needs to put this behind her once and for all.

"You wanna hang around a while longer, babe?"

"Nah, I think I've done enough damage for one night."

Doug and Meg decide to head out too, so the six of us walk out together. We drop Melissa off, then drive home. Judd says good night and walks over to his farm. We take the dogs out to the backyard and sit down at the patio table while they run and play.

"Babe, we need to talk."

"You sound serious."

"I am. What happened tonight, while deserved, isn't the answer."

"Maybe, but it felt damn good."

"I get that, but it can also lead you down a dangerous road."

"You're right, and to tell you the truth, I can't say I enjoyed it."

"Good. Now, how about we put it behind us?"

"What'd you have in mind?"

I call the dogs inside, then throw Lexi over my shoulder and carry her to the bedroom. I can't get her naked fast enough. I lay her down and join her. She reaches her arms out, wrapping them around me when I lean over her. I kiss her with passion as I spread her legs. My fingers find her pussy and fuck, she's wet. I hear her moan as I pleasure her.

I work my way down her beautiful body, my mouth tasting every inch of her silky skin. I know where she wants my mouth most, so I skip down to her legs. I suck the inside of each thigh, just close enough to her pussy to drive her wild. After I've teased her enough, I spread her legs wide. Fuck, she looks so good lying there naked. I run my tongue up and down, stopping to suck on her clit. She runs her fingers through my hair, holding my head in place. I feel her body quake as she explodes. I hear her screaming my name as she comes hard.

She pushes me onto my back and climbs on top. It feels so good when she takes me inside. I hold her hips as she sits up straight, giving me a full view of her sexy curves. She rides me hard. She bucks as she comes undone again. Feeling her love rain down on me, I empty myself inside her. She collapses onto my chest and I wrap my arms around her. She lowers her head and kisses me, her tongue dancing with mine. She moves next to me and drifts off to sleep.

The next morning, we're sitting on the patio drinking coffee, watching our furry kids romp in the backyard. The sky is a beautiful shade of blue and the summer sun shines bright, though not as bright as the beauty sitting next to me. I think back to last night and how much fun we had in bed, and a wide smile fills my face. I love this woman so much, and for the first time, I can see myself married.

We're in a beautiful field with vibrant colored wildflowers. Dave is in a tux and Maggie has a small white veil on. I can picture myself on bended knee in front of Lexi, tears streaming down her face. The dogs are sitting on either side of me. I open a small red velvet box and show her a ring that makes her jaw drop. I hear her saying yes. We embrace and kiss before I lay her down and make love to her right there in the field.

"DUDE!"

I look over and see Dean sitting there with Lexi, amused looks on both of their faces.

Chapter Three

"Dean stopped by to find out if we heard the show on Octane last night. We were chatting away about it and spent the entire time staring at our flower garden." I said.

"Sorry, babe, I zoned out."

"Lexi told me you heard the song on the way to her reunion," Dean said. "How was that?"

"Ask my badass woman."

Dean looks over, so I fill him in on the events from last night. He laughs as he listens to what I did and said to Bryan.

"You definitely remind me of Alex."

"Thanks. I'm not proud of some of it, but I needed to do it."

"I get that. On to a happier topic. The response from listeners has been positive. Xander was checking out their social media pages and saw lots of people saying they love your voice. He wants you to record a couple more songs."

"Babe, that's incredible." Damien smiles.

"He also wants you, Damien. He thinks you and Lexi doing a duet would rock."

"Babe, what do you think?"

"Count me in."

I can't believe I just said that with no hesitation. Before I met Damien, the thought of doing anything outside of my comfort zone would have been a hard pass. Now, I want to do it all. Of course, more than anything, I want to do him, but there'll be time for that later. Damien's phone rings, so he excuses himself.

"Xander's excited to work with you. Is this something you'd want to pursue beyond what we're doing?" Dean asks.

"I never gave it any thought. I don't want to be in IT the rest of my life."

"What do you want to do?"

"I want to open a bookstore/cafe with a twist. Instead of just coffee, I want to serve alcohol, so it would be adults only."

"You could add open mic nights too, so you could sing."

"You really have me thinking."

"Thinking about what?" Damien asks.

"I was telling Dean about my dream job."

"I hope this isn't a sore subject." Dean said.

"Not at all," Damien said.

"Then think it over. I gotta run, taking Alex out for lunch. I'll be in touch about recording."

"Thanks. Have fun at lunch."

"So, babe, tell me the truth. If you could quit your job today and open your bookstore, would you?" He asks.

"Without hesitation."

"Then why don't you?"

"I can't just quit and have no income."

"Babe, we can do this."

"We?"

"I want to do this together." He smiles.

"I need some time to think about it."

"I understand. I think, though, that you need a break. Can you take some time off?"

"What'd you have in mind?"

"A trip. Ever been to Maine?"

"No, but I've always wanted to. What about the dogs?"

"Judd said he would watch them any time we needed."

"I'll check with my boss tomorrow."

"Great. I can't promise we'll actually do any sightseeing."

"And why is that? If I go, I want to see things." I smile.

"You mean things other than my dick?"

"Contrary to popular belief, there are other things that excite me besides what's in your pants!"

"Is that so?"

I stick my tongue out at him. "Yep."

Damien grabs me and tickles my stomach. I double over, laughing, and pull away from him. I take off running and he chases me. I run until I reach the weeping willow tree in the back corner of his yard. I hide behind the tree as he reaches it. I keep running around the tree with him hot on my tail. He dekes and catches me, pulling us both to the ground. Within seconds, he's leaning over me, kissing me hard. We lie there holding each other until we hear a loud throat clear.

"Get a room, lovebirds."

Melissa is standing there smiling at us. Damien gets up and helps me up. We're both panting from running and kissing.

"Came to see if you're okay after last night, but I clearly had nothing to worry about."

"I'm not proud of some of the stuff I did and said, but I feel like it's the closure I needed."

"I get that. I also stopped by for some girl talk, unless you guys have plans."

"Tell you what, I'll take the dogs down to the park and give you girls some alone time."

"Thanks," Melissa said.

I see tears forming in her eyes as she sits down. Damien ushers the dogs inside, and a few minutes later, I hear his car backing out of the driveway.

"You want something to drink?"

"Coffee, please."

"Be right back."

After I return with two cups of coffee and some cookies, I sit down at the table with my best friend. She grabs a cookie but doesn't eat it. Now I know something's wrong. She's always been the female version of Cookie Monster from Sesame Street.

"Talk to me. What's going on?"

"I'm tired of being alone. I know I shouldn't be complaining. I have a great job, I own a home, I have the best friend in the world, even so, something's missing. I'm tired of sleeping alone every night."

I place my hand over hers. "I understand. You're the most amazing person I've ever known. You deserve someone to worship at your feet."

"Hell, I'll just take someone who'll touch my lady-bits. I'm beyond ready to break things off with BOB."

"What about a certain sexy cowboy?"

"Oh yeah, the cowboy in his dirty t-shirts and jeans dating the executive VP in her business suits. Sounds like something that only exists in those steamy romance novels. Except that he's such a gentleman, he probably wouldn't act like those naughty boys in the books."

"I think you're wrong. I feel there's something hiding under all that charm."

"I'm not so sure. He doesn't even show any skin other than his face and a bit of neck."

Before I can respond, I see movement out of the corner of my eye. I lose the ability to speak, and all I can do is tap Melissa's arm and point. Her eyes follow my gaze, and I see her jaw drop open. She slides her chair next to mine. We huddle together, our eyes fixated on the farm next door.

The most beautiful white stallion gallops around the fenced in area. The horse's beauty is nothing compared to the rider. We're frozen in our chairs, watching him. Tight Wranglers cover his ass. A pair of well-worn brown boots is tucked into the stirrups, and a tan cowboy sits atop his head. And that's all. He's shirtless, and holy shit! Damien's face floats into my head and I recover. Melissa, not so much.

She can't take her eyes off of him. Judd has muscles for days. Arms, chest, back, neck, you name it, it's muscular. I can only imagine what he's packing in those jeans. I stop myself, remembering that I already have a man. Besides, it's always been rock stars that make me drool. I hear Melissa sigh, her eyes still following the cowboy's every move.

"You wanna ride him, don't you?"

"Hell yeah. Look at those muscles."

I hear a couple of barks. Dave and Maggie run over to the fence and bark at Judd. He rides over and Melissa almost falls out of her chair. I try not to laugh at Miss 'I Always Have my Shit Together.' I've never seen her react like this to a man.

Chapter Four

Damien

I walk over to Lexi and whisper in her ear.

"Looks like someone wants to take a ride."

She elbows me in the side. Judd jumps the fence and walks over to where we're all standing. I watch Melissa, waiting for her to pass out cold, but she pulls herself together.

"Howdy, ma'am," Judd said, tipping his hat toward Melissa.

"Hey." Melissa turns to Lexi. "I gotta run. Thanks for this."

Judd rides off as Lexi walks Melissa to her car. I can hear their conversation.

"I've never seen you act like that, girl."

"Did you see him? Holy fuck, he's sexy."

"Want me to put in a good word?"

"One word and I'll kill you." Melissa says.

"But you said you were tired of being alone."

"I know, but please, just promise me, not a damn word."

"I promise."

I sit down at the table, waiting for Lexi to return.

"Do I wanna know what that was all about?" I ask.

"Probably not, but I'm gonna tell you, anyway."

"Would it be okay if I told you something first?"

"Sure. What's on your mind?"

"The phone call I got when Dean was here."

"Talk to me."

"It was Mr. Hyman, the music teacher I told you about. He wants to see me. Something sounded off, and I'm worried. I think I need to fly back to California for a few days. Would you mind?" I ask.

"Of course not."

"Thanks, babe."

"Of course, and you know I will take great care of Dave."

"Never a doubt, babe."

"If it's okay, I might ask Melissa to stay here while you're gone."

"Are you sure she can handle being that close to Judd?"

"I hope so."

I run in the house and grab my laptop, so I can check on flights. I find something where I can leave tomorrow, so I buy my ticket and let Lexi know.

"I found a flight leaving around noon tomorrow. I'm sorry it's so soon."

"Don't be. I understand how important this is to you. We'll be fine." Lexi smiles.

"Since you'll be at work, I'll have Judd drive me to the airport."

"Are you sure? I can take tomorrow off."

"No need. Besides, I want you to go to work so you can get time off for our trip."

"Okay. I'm getting hungry. You want some lunch?"

"Sounds great."

I follow Lexi inside, my eyes never leaving that sexy round ass of hers. I love having my hands on her ass while she's bouncing on my dick. Just like that, he awakens and stirs in my pants.

"What do you want to eat?" she asks me.

I back her against the counter and press my body against hers. "You, babe."

Before she can answer, I crush my lips to hers and jam my tongue

15

into her mouth. She opens for me and intertwines her tongue with mine. I lift her up onto the counter. Fuck, I want this woman. I lift her shirt over her head and toss it aside. I lightly bite each of her soft shoulders as she runs her fingers through my hair. She moans as I suck on her neck and work my way down to her breasts. I lift her off the counter and carry her to our bedroom. She wraps her arms around my neck and lays her head on my shoulder.

I lay her down on the bed and remove the rest of her clothes. She's so beautiful. She sits up and grabs the belt loops on my jeans. I move between her legs. Her hands slide under my shirt and lift it off. She leans forward and runs her tongue down my chest and down to my stomach. I inhale the sweet smell of her strawberry shampoo as her tongue explores my body.

She opens my jeans and finds out that I'm going commando. My erection springs out of my jeans. She opens her mouth and slides her soft lips up and down my shaft as her fingers tickle my balls. She spreads her legs wide and grabs my hand. She guides my fingers inside her. She moans as she sucks my cock. The vibrations drive me crazy. I need to be inside her.

"Babe, lay back and spread those legs. I need to fuck you. NOW!"

She does as she's told and I lay on top of her, my hands on each side of her, so she's not bearing my full weight. I slide into her with ease, thrusting hard. She wraps her legs around my waist, holding me inside her as I pound that sweet pussy hard. Her fingers run through my hair, rake my back, and take up residence on my ass. She squeezes hard as we fuck until I lose all control and empty myself inside her. I lay next to her, and tease her clit with my fingers until her body quakes. She moans as I bring her to orgasm.

"Mmm, what was that for?" she asks.

"Something to think about while I'm gone, babe."

"I love you."

"Love you too."

I wake up an hour later, with Lexi still in my arms. My stomach rumbles, but I don't have the heart to wake her. I wait until I feel her stir, then ask her about dinner.

"Hungry, babe?"

"Famished after that hot fuck."

"How about a shower, then we go out?"

"I'd love to."

I follow my sexy woman to the bathroom. I've come to love walking behind her. She has the sexiest ass of any woman I've ever seen. We get into the shower and I grab her shower gel. My hands explore her sexy body as I wash her. I'm having a hell of a time keeping my dick under control. Watching the water cascade down her silky skin is more than I can handle and I'm hard.

"Babe, get against the wall and hold on."

I get behind her, grab her waist, and enter her from behind. I fuck her pussy hard, rubbing her clit with my thumb until we both quake from powerful orgasms. We finish our shower, then head down to the local pizza joint for dinner. After we're done, we take the dogs to the dog park and let them play. We sit down on a bench and I put my arm around her.

"I'm gonna miss you, babe."

"I'll miss you too."

When the dogs are done playing, they walk over and lay down in front of us. Lexi and I put their leashes on them and head home so I can pack. Once I'm done, we camp out in front of the TV. I want to spend as much time as possible with Lexi before I have to leave. We stay up as late as possible, not wanting to use our time together sleeping, but Lexi has to work in the morning. We enjoy breakfast together before she has to head out.

"Have a safe flight. Call when you can. I love you."

"I love you, babe. I'll let you know after I talk to Mr. Hyman how long I'm going to stay."

I watch her back out of the driveway and I miss her already. When it's time, I head over to Judd's with my luggage and we head to the airport. I head inside after he drops me off and I get in the security line. Once I'm through, I walk to the gate and wait for my flight to be called. All I can think about is Lexi. I'm going to miss having her warm body next to mine in bed. After a while, it's my turn to board, so I head down the tunnel and get myself situated. I watch the ground disappear as we climb higher, and I can't help but wonder what California has in store for me.

Chapter Five

Lexi

I pull into the parking lot at work and sigh. I miss Damien. I head inside and walk to my desk. I see a note from my boss asking me to come to his office when I arrive. After I put my stuff on my desk, I walk down the hall to his office and knock on the door.

"Come in," Mark says.

I walk in and take a seat in the chair in front of his desk.

"Thanks for coming in, Lexi. I wish I didn't have to do this, but we've been bought."

"Isn't that good news?"

"For the company, yes however, the new owner is bringing in their own employees."

"What?"

"I'm sorry, Lexi. You know how much I value your work, but they have eliminated your job. You will receive severance pay. Because of the circumstances, you'll receive two weeks of pay for each year of service." He sighs.

"But, Mark. I've been here for 25 years and I've done a good job."

"I know that, and had it been up to me, you'd still be here. But they can bring their own people in for less money."

I feel tears threatening to spill over, and the last thing I want is Mark to see that. I take a deep breath, trying to hold them in.

"When's my last day?"

"Friday. Unless you want to leave sooner. I'm leaving that up to you. I hope you know I'm sick about this."

"I appreciate that. If it's okay with you, I just want to leave today, but I really don't want anyone to know."

"I brought in donuts and bagels, so I'll put them out and call everyone to the break room. That should give you enough time."

"Thanks, Mark,I should thank you. I've been thinking about giving notice, as I want to open a bookstore. I was on the fence about the risk, but now that this has happened, I'm going to do it." I smile at him.

"Keep me posted and I'll do what I can to help."

"I appreciate that. Is there somewhere I can get some boxes?"

"I'll have one of the warehouse guys bring some here."

"Okay."

After I sign the required paperwork and hand my ID badge to him, Mark calls down and requests some boxes. Once they arrive, he puts out the food, then calls the rest of the staff to the break room. I quickly pack up my belongings and take the boxes down to my car before anyone sees me. What happened today hits me hard as I drive home, especially since Damien isn't there. I go inside and collapse on the couch. Maggie jumps up next to me and Dave lays at my feet. I pet them both, grateful for their company.

After I shower and change, I take the dogs out back to play. I grab my latest read, Mission Promiscuous, the phenomenal debut by Lala Montgomery. The book is hotter than hell, especially Elijah Adler. Fuck, I miss Damien. I hope he's having a better time in LA than I am here. I'll be glad when Melissa gets here later.

When the dogs finish playing, I take them inside and get their dinner ready. They're just finishing when Melissa gets here, pizza and wine in hand.

"I'm glad to see you," I say to my friend.

"What's wrong? Is it Damien?"

"No. I got to work this morning and got some interesting news. Mark called me into his office to let me know the company was bought out. The new owners are bringing in their own people, so they eliminated my job. I got a good severance package, but it still hurts. Mark felt terrible, but his hands were tied."

"I'm so sorry, sweetie. Did you call Damien?"

"No, I didn't want to bother him with this until I know what's going on with his former teacher."

"You're a good woman. What are you going to do now?" She asks.

"I've been thinking for a while about resigning and opening the bookstore I always wanted to. Damien has been trying to talk me into it, and now, what the hell? They decided for me. I'm going to wait until he gets back before I do anything."

"It's going to be amazing."

"Thanks, Mel."

"For now, though, let's eat way too much pizza and drink way too much wine."

"I like the way you think."

We carry everything out to the living room. I pull up Friends on Netflix. Friends is one of my favorite comfort shows. We sit and laugh our asses off, despite the hundreds of times we've seen these episodes. We finished the entire pizza and two bottles of wine. I'm still missing Damien, but it helps to have Melissa here. I hear my cell ring and see a handsome face appear on the screen.

"Hello."

"Hey, babe."

"I just got to the hotel. I'm meeting Mr. Hyman for dinner, and wanted to call you before I head out. Everything good there?" He asks.

"Yep. Mel and I just had some pizza and a bit of wine."

"Sounds like you had more than a bit."

"Okay, two bottles."

"That's my girl. How are the dogs?"

"They're sound asleep. I plan on joining them soon." I laugh.

"Okay. I'll call you tomorrow. I should know when I'll be home. I love you."

"I love you too."

"Good night, babe."

"Good night."

After we disconnect, I clean up the living room. Between the wine and what happened at work today, I'm barely able to keep my eyes. Melissa yawns.

"I'm heading to bed after I take the dogs out," I say to Mel.

"Me too."

We take the dogs out to the backyard and once we bring them back inside, I lock up. Melissa heads into the guest room while I climb into my bed. The bed seems huge without Damien next to me. I can smell his shower gel on the sheets and I miss him. I lie there and think about all the dirty fun we've had here. I feel my eyelids getting heavy and that's the last thing I remember until I hear Maggie barking the next morning.

I get up and take both dogs out back before they wake Melissa. They run around a bit, then do their business. I take them back inside and get their breakfast ready. While they're eating, I start a pot of coffee. Mel shuffles out a little while later, eyes half-closed. I pour two cups of coffee and hand her one.

"Do you want breakfast?" I ask.

"I can grab something on my way to the office if you don't feel like cooking."

"Up to you, but I'm going to cook for myself, so I don't mind."

"Okay, thanks. Mind if I grab a shower while you're getting it ready?"

"Not at all."

She downs the rest of her coffee, then heads off to the shower. I grab what I need to make French toast and get the griddle out. Melissa comes out to the kitchen just as I'm finishing up. I make up two plates and pour two more cups of coffee. We decide to eat on the back patio, so the dogs can play a bit.

"What are you going to do today?"

"I might drive around and look for a location for the book store. Otherwise, not much."

"When I'm done with work, I'll grab food and then be over. I have enough clothes with me for a couple more days, depending on how long Damien is gone."

"Thanks for being here."

"Love you, girl."

"Love you too."

We're just finishing breakfast when we see Judd.

"Look, it's your boyfriend."

"Shut up!"

"Mel and Judd sitting in a tree."

"How old are you?"

We both laugh out loud. Judd sees us and walks over.

"Good Morning, ladies."

"Hey, Judd," I say. Melissa says nothing, just sits and stares. "She needs more coffee," I say.

Judd smiles and waves, then gets back to work. Melissa is frozen in her chair, still just staring at him. I can't help but laugh at the effect he has on her. I call the dogs in and put our dishes in the sink. Melissa gathers up what she needs for work and heads out. After I clean up the dishes, I watch some TV. Mid-morning, I take the dogs to the park then drive around scoping out places where I could open a bookstore. I'm just pulling into the driveway when my phone rings. Damien.

Chapter Six

Damien

"Hello," Lexi says.

"Babe. I just finished lunch with Mr. Hyman."

"What's wrong? I can hear it in your voice."

"He's got cancer. Terminal. He wanted to tell me in person, but he's too sick to travel."

"Oh no. I'm so sorry, baby."

"Me too. I'm flying back home tomorrow."

"So soon?" She asks me.

"He doesn't want me to stay. He wants me to remember him as he is now, still looking like the man I remember."

"I guess it makes sense. If he changes his mind or you decide to stay longer, you know I completely understand."

"I know, babe. I thought about staying anyway, but I want to respect his wishes after everything he did to help me when I was a kid."

"You're a good man, baby. I'm so lucky I found you."

"I'm going to have dinner and spend some time with him tonight, then fly out in the morning. He went home after lunch to take a nap." I sigh.

"I wish I could give you a hug. I can't imagine how hard this is for you."

"I'll take you up on that tomorrow. Can you do me a favor and make sure Mel is gone when I get home? I know that sounds rude, but I just want to be alone with you."

"I totally understand. It's not rude."

"Thanks, babe. I'm going to grab a shower and get ready for dinner. I'm taking an early flight, so I should be home in the afternoon."

"Have a good time tonight. I love you."

"I love you more, babe." I reply.

After we disconnect, I grab a shower and get ready for dinner. But, can I really be ready for this? This could be the last time I ever see him alive. I'm determined to honor his wishes, but I feel guilty for not staying. My head is a mess right now. I need to calm down before I pick him up for dinner. I decide to take a walk around the hotel grounds, wishing Lexi and the dogs were with me. I walk until it's time to leave for dinner. I get to his house, and he's waiting out front. He walks over to my rental car and gets in.

"Hey, Mr. Hyman."

"I have a request, if it's okay."

"Sure. What?"

"I know you're being respectful calling me Mr. Hyman, but would you mind calling me by my first name?" He smiles at me.

"Of course. Hey, Jack."

"Thank you."

"Where do you want to eat tonight?"

"I'd love to go to our favorite Chinese restaurant."

"I remember exactly where."

I drive to the restaurant Jack always took me to. I try desperately not to break down, thinking about all the wonderful memories I have with him. He was more of a father to me than the shithead that donated his sperm to my mom. We pull into the parking lot and head inside. After we're seated, we decide on our meals.

"I have one more request for after dinner," Jack says.

"Anything."

"I want to hear you sing one last time. I hope you don't mind, but I signed you up for an extended spot at one of the local clubs."

"I don't mind at all. But you need to pick the songs."

"I made a list."

I smile as our waiter approaches and takes our order. While we wait for the food, we talk some more.

"So, tell me more about Lexi. Your face lights up every time you mention her. She must be special."

"That she is, and she doesn't know it. Her last boyfriend treated her like shit. She's beautiful, smart, and she has a heart of gold. She works in IT and she can also sing. She reminds me of Janis Joplin. I have a cute picture of her with her dog, Maggie and Dave."

I grab my phone and show Jack the picture.

"You're right, she is beautiful. That smile is infectious. How did you two meet?"

"We met at the dog park. Dave kinda knocked her on her butt. Lucky for me, she also has a lab, so she knows what they can be like. We had a good laugh about it. It wasn't long afterwards that we started dating."

"Is she the one?"

"I really think she is. I've never felt this way before. I'm definitely in love with her. For the first time in my life, the thought of marriage doesn't scare me."

"Then please, don't wait. I don't need to tell you how brief life can be."

I feel tears prick my eyes and I fight them off. I'm not sure what to say, so I just nod.

"No pity, no sadness. I want to have fun tonight."

He always could read me. I couldn't have asked for a better mentor and role model. A few minutes later, our food comes. I'm glad to see he still has his appetite. We both finish up, the waiter clears our plates and drops off the check. Of course, Jack won't let me pay. Once we're back in the car, he asks me if I remember the club where he used to take me.

"Of course. Getting to see all those amazing bands before they hit big was one highlight of my youth."

"Great. That's where I booked you to sing."

"I can't wait."

We drive to the club, neither of us saying much. The bouncer knows him well and takes him to a table right down front. The owner, a man I remember as Billy, comes over with a pitcher of beer.

"Hey, Jack.:"

"Hi. Do you remember the student I used to bring in here?"

"Damien, right?"

"Yep. Well, this is him all grown up."

"Nice to see you again. I'm looking forward to hearing you sing tonight."

I see the way Billy looks at Jack and I realize something. They're in love. Jack never spoke much about his personal life, and now I know why. The close-minded parents would have tried to get him fired. I never understood that mentality, and I'm glad Jack trusted me enough to reveal his secret to me.

"How long have you two been together?"

"We met not long after you graduated high school."

"I'm so happy. It's easy to see how much you love each other. I hope you put something special on my playlist."

"I did. 'Still Loving You' was our song. Our first date was a Scorpions concert." He smiles.

"I'm honored to sing that for you both. Is it okay for me to dedicate it to you?"

"Thank you. And yes, everyone at the club knows about us."

Billy walks on stage and grabs the microphone.

"We have a very special treat for you tonight. Our own Damien St. James is visiting us from his new home out east. Please join me in welcoming him to the stage."

I was met with loud applause as I walked onto the stage. Billy handed me the microphone and shook my hand. He joined Jack at our table. I saved their song for the last. I made my way through the rest of the playlist.

"My last song of the night is dedicated to two very special people. Billy and Jack, this one's for you."

My eyes fill with tears as I watch Billy and Jack. It breaks my heart that Billy is going to lose him. I finish the song. I thank the crowd and return to the table. Jack and I ended up staying until last call. I hug them both goodbye in the parking lot. I slip Billy my phone number so he can keep me posted. I wait in the parking lot until they're gone, then I drive to my hotel. I'm glad I'll be back in Lexi's arms tomorrow. I need her now more than ever.

I set the alarm on my phone and head to bed. The next morning, I pack up, check out, and head to the airport. I can't wait to get home and just hold Lexi. I don't know what I'd do without her. As I'm in my seat waiting for the plane to take off, I think about what Jack said. I think it might be time to grab Melissa and take her to a jewelry store to help me pick out a ring.

Chapter Seven

Lexi

I'm awakened by a text alert on my phone. It's from Damien letting me know his flight information. He ends the message with eggplant and cat emojis. Now I'm especially looking forward to him getting home! I grab a shower, get dressed, then take the dogs out to do their business. They stare at me while I get their breakfast. I put the bowls down and it's a race to see who finishes first. I grab myself a bowl of cereal and coffee. I take the dogs to the backyard and enjoy breakfast on the patio. After I eat, I finish Mission Promiscuous. I can't wait to read her next book!

When the dogs finish running, we all head back inside. I do some quick cleaning before Damien gets home, then run out to the grocery store so I can have a nice dinner ready for him tonight. I'm looking forward to spending a night alone, some of which I expect will not require clothing. Just the thought of being naked with him gets me riled up. I make a mental note to stay away from any phallic-shaped food when I go to the store.

I decide on lasagna, so I grab what I need and head back home. I get everything ready and in the fridge, so all I have to do is put it in the oven when he gets home. His flight should land in about two hours, so I get restless. I load the dogs up in the car and drive to Philly. I get to the airport about half an hour before he's scheduled to land and park in the cell phone lot. I'm checking social media when my phone rings.

"Hey, Mr. Sexy."

"Babe, I just got my luggage, if you want to head over."

"On my way."

I drive over to the Southwest Airlines pickup area. The dogs see him before I do and they go crazy in the back seat. I pop the trunk and get out of the car. Damien greets me with a big hug and a passionate kiss.

"Damn, I missed your soft lips, babe."

"I've missed your dick."

"I have a feeling you'll be reunited later." He smirks at me.

"Mmmm, can't wait."

"Want me to drive back?"

"Either way is fine."

Damien walks to the driver's side, so I walk around and get in the passenger's side. Damien's hungry, so we grab lunch and find a parking lot so we can eat. Once we get home, Damien grabs a shower, so I decide to surprise him. I quickly strip and lay down in bed. He walks into the bedroom with only a towel wrapped around his waist and my mouth waters. I get up and walk over to him, his eyes scanning my naked body. I open his towel and let it fall to the floor. He pulls me close and I can feel how hard his dick is. He backs me against the wall and kisses me hard. I feel my knees go weak and I have to put my hands on his broad shoulders.

"Spread those sexy legs," he says.

I do as I'm told. I watch him get down on his knees. His mouth quickly finds my pussy, and he licks. I brace myself against the wall as his tongue works his magic. He sucks my clit hard and I almost go down. Fuck, it feels so good.

"Babe, turn around and face the wall."

I turn around and feel Damien's hands on my waist. He presses himself into me and slides his dick inside my pussy from behind. Nobody's ever fucked me this way before, and it's driving me wild. He slides his hands up to my boobs and massages them while he pounds me hard. He slides a hand down and circles my clit with his thumb. I can't believe I'm still able to stand. My entire body is on fire and tingling. I hear a low growl and feel Damien empty inside me.

"Don't move."

I stay against the wall as Damien walks over to the night table next to the bed. I hear a buzzing sound when he returns, and I brace myself again. He presses the vibrator against my clit. Within minutes, my body quakes as I come undone.

"Oh, fuck, baby, so damn amazing."

My legs are shaking, so Damien helps me over to the bed. We lay down together, and he pulls me close. He pulls the covers up as we hold each other. I feel something dripping on my shoulder. I look up and tears are spilling out of my love's eyes. My heart breaks as I gently wipe his cheek.

"I'm here if you want to talk," I whisper.

"It's so fucking unfair. A great man like Jack gets cancer and an asshole like my dad gets to take up space."

I feel him squeeze me tighter, like he's holding on for dear life. This is a side of him he hadn't shown me until today. I didn't know it could be possible, but I love him even more.

"I wish I had an answer."

"He said something to me at dinner, and I can't get it out of my head."

"Tell me, please."

"Okay, but know this is not me trying to scare you."

"Got it."

"He asked me if I thought you were the one, and I said yes. I told him that for the first time in my life, thinking about settling down doesn't scare me. He told me not to wait, as time isn't guaranteed."

"He's right, but please, don't do anything that makes you uneasy. We're amazing the way we are." I smile.

"Yes we are. But hypothetically if I were to ask."

"I wouldn't run for the hills."

"Good to know. I sure wouldn't mind fucking on a hill, though. I could get you into some interesting positions."

"Is that all you think about, Mr. Horny?"

"Oh, please, Little Miss Lusty."

Something about that strikes me, and I laugh so hard, I snort. That sets Damien off, and we're lying there laughing like a pair of idiots. I'm laughing so hard, my stomach and face hurt.

"You always know exactly what I need, babe."

"I aim to please."

"So, do you have to go back to work tomorrow, or did you take another day off?"

"Um, about that."

"What?"

"I don't have a job to go back to."

"What?"

"Monday morning, I got to work and saw a note to see my boss. A competitor bought out, and they eliminated my position." I tell him.

"Why didn't you call me?"

"You had enough going on."

"Thanks, but I would have been there for you."

"I know, but I wanted you to focus on Jack. Mel was here, and trust me, Maggie and Dave helped, too. But now, I'm free to open the bookstore. I spent yesterday driving around, looking for viable locations."

"Find anything?"

"Some possibilities, but I would want to see the inside."

"We could do that together."

"I would love to."

We spend the next month looking at places for the bookstore, but none of them strike my fancy. We stop and grab dinner to take home. After we eat, we feed the dogs and take them to the dog park to play. We've just headed to bed when Damien's cell rings.

"Hello?"

I watch his face crumble as his body shakes. Tears spill out of his eyes. My heart breaks for him as tears slide down my cheeks. I reach out and wrap my arms around him.

Chapter Eight

Damien

"Oh, Billy, I'm so very sorry."

"Yes, keep me posted."

"Take care of yourself."

I disconnect the phone and pull Lexi close.

"It was like he was waiting for my visit, so he could say goodbye." I sigh.

"I'm so sorry, baby."

"Thanks, babe."

"What can I do?"

"For now, please just let me hold you."

She nestles into my arms. We're still naked. The feel of her skin against mine brings me the comfort I desperately need. This is one of those times that I'm glad she's not one of those women who never shuts up. I focus on her breathing and her heartbeat. I love this woman so much.

"I'm exhausted, babe."

"Okay. I'll take the dogs out and lock up."

"Thanks, babe."

I lie there and wait for Lexi to come back. She removes her robe and crawls into bed. All I want is to hold her, so I pull her in close and pull the covers up. She looks up at me and kisses me softly. That's the last thing I remember until the sunlight streams into our windows in the morning. I reach over and the bed is empty. I walk out to the kitchen and see Lexi standing at the stove. I see some kind of meat sitting on a plate on the counter, though I don't know what.

"Good Morning, baby. Did you sleep okay?"

"Yeah."

"I'm almost done with the eggs."

"What's on the plate?" I ask her.

"Scrapple."

"What's that? I've never heard of it."

"It's mostly found in Pennsylvania, so not surprised. It's pork. Try it. I promise you'll like it."

"You really want me to put that meat in my mouth?"

"If you expect me to put your meat in my mouth, you'll damn well do it!"

"Well, when you put it that way."

I take a small bite and I'm surprised. It's actually tasty. But do I want to admit to Lexi that she was right? Well, if it means getting her pretty, full lips wrapped around my cock, hell yeah.

"It's not bad."

"Thanks. Some people slice it thicker, but I prefer the thinner cut."

"Just remember what you told me. I'm going to expect those lips around my meat later."

"We'll see."

"Oh, is that so?"

She smiles at me for a minute, then her face turns serious.

"Are you sure you're okay?"

"I am. Of course, I'm sad, but he was suffering."

"You're right. My heart breaks for Billy."

"Mine too. In the time I spent with them, it was easy to see how much they loved each other. Can I ask you something?"

"Of course."

"Will you come to LA with me for the funeral? Judd always said he would watch the dogs if we needed."

"Absolutely. I want to be there for whatever you need."

"Thanks, babe. Billy's going to let me know once he's made the arrangements."

We finish breakfast and I help Lexi clean up. We take the dogs out back to let them play for a while. I'm feeling restless, so I walk down to the willow tree and sit down. I see Lexi get up and head down. She sits next to me and lays her head on my shoulder. I'd never be able to get through this without her. I lay down in the grass and pull her down next to me. I wrap my arms around her as she lays her head on my chest. We gaze up at the bright blue sky and just hold each other. I'm overwhelmed by the peace that comes from holding her. After a little more playing, the dogs come over and lay with us. All I can think about is what a perfect family we are.

The next morning, I tell Lexi I have an appointment and I head out. I pull into a parking lot around the corner and call Melissa, who agrees to meet me after spending five minutes squealing into the phone. I drive to my destination and park behind the store. I'm already inside looking when Melissa walks in, a huge grin on her face.

"I'm so excited. Thanks for including me." She squeals at me.

"Just promise you won't tell her. I have a fun proposal planned."

"I promise."

"You know her taste. What would she like?"

I watch Melissa walking around looking. She stops in front of the case and waves me over.

"This one. I remember her showing something similar in a magazine."

The sales clerk removes the ring so I can look closer. It has a one-carat round diamond in the middle, with a smaller round diamond on each side. The ring is simple and beautiful, not flashy, just like Lexi.

"I'll take it. Melissa, do you know her size?"

"We're the same, so you can measure mine."

"Mr. St. James, it will take us about a week to size the ring. We'll contact you when it's done. We just need to complete your paperwork and the payment, then you can be on your way."

"I need to head back to work. Let me know if I can help with the proposal."

"Will do. Thanks for the help."

"My pleasure."

Once I finish signing everything and paying for the ring, I head home, noting some places I want to send Lexi on her quest. I plan to end things at the dog park. If not for that place, we may have never met. Of course, I will have the dogs as part of the proposal. I can't wait. Now I just have to act normal until the ring comes in. I just pull into the driveway when my phone rings. I see Billy's name pop up on the screen.

"Hello."

"It's Billy. I have the funeral information."

"Okay. One sec, let me grab paper."

I open the glove box and grab the paper and pen Lexi put in there. You should always have something to write on and write with, she told me.

"Go ahead."

"The viewing is this Thursday night, followed by a celebration of life on Friday."

"Thanks. I'll check flights and plan to arrive Wednesday at the latest."

"Jack had a request, if you're willing."

"What request?"

"He wanted you to sing at the service."

"I'm honored. I will absolutely do it."

"Thank you. Let me know once you arrive."

"Will do. Lexi will make this trip with me."

"I look forward to meeting her."

"Take care, and we'll see you in a couple of days."

"Goodbye, Damien."

"Bye, Billy."

I disconnect the phone and head inside. I can see Lexi out back with the dogs, her nose in a book. I hope it's another dirty one! I love watching her do, well, pretty much anything. She looks up when she hears the sliding glass door open.

"Oooh, Mr. Sexy, do I have some fun ideas for the bedroom," she says, waving the book.

She's reading the newest by local author Eden Mitchell. I heard her books are super-smutty and my dick twitches, wondering what my babe has running through her pretty head right now!

"I hate to dampen the mood, as I'm intrigued by what you might plan, but Billy called as I was pulling into the driveway."

"How's he doing?"

"As well as he can. He let me know the funeral arrangements, so I need to book our travel. Could you do me a favor?"

"Of course, what?"

"Could you run over and ask Judd if he wouldn't mind keeping the dogs for a couple of days? It would be from Wednesday to Sunday. Or maybe we should have Melissa ask."

"Ha, ha! I'll be right back."

I open my laptop and wait for it to boot up. I watch Lexi's sexy hips sway as she walks towards Judd's house and I'm hard. Wait until she gets back! In the meantime, I get our travel all booked up and send a text with the information to Billy. I'm relieved Lexi agreed to go with me. I don't know that I could face this alone. I look out and see her at the far corner of the property chatting with Judd, both dogs by her side, and I can't help but smile. I love that I'm going to be waking up to her for the rest of my life.

Chapter Nine

Lexi

I see Judd towards the back of his property, so I walk back, two piles of fur hot on my heels. I stop and lean on the fence, watching him work for a few minutes before he sees me. My mind goes to Melissa and how badly she wants that sexy cowboy, even if she doesn't realize it or won't admit it.

"Howdy, ma'am," he says, tipping his hat.

Normally, I despise being called ma'am, but there's something about the way he says it...

"Hello, Judd. Damien asked me to walk back and ask a favor of you." I ask sweetly.

"What, darlin'?"

"Would you be willing to dog-sit these two from Wednesday through Sunday?"

"It would be my pleasure. Is that for the services?"

"Yes, Damien got a call this morning. He's stayed back to book our travel."

"I can't imagine how hard this must be for him."

"It is. I just keep letting him know I'm there."

"You're a good woman. Glad he found you."

"Why, thank you."

"Speaking of good women, how's Melissa doing?"

Was that a glint I saw in those coffee-colored eyes? Wait until I tell Damien! I try not to giggle when I respond.

"She's well. I need to have her over again soon!"

"That sounds fun. Maybe when you and Damien are back home."

"I'll let Damien know. Thank you so much for helping us like this."

"Any time, darlin'."

Judd heads back to work, so I walk back home so I can fill Damien in. Maggie and Dave stop to roll around in the grass while I join Damien at the table.

"Maybe we should join them," I say with a wink.

"Naughty, naughty, babe."

"Judd said he'd be happy to watch the dogs. He also asked me how Melissa was. I swore I saw a gleam in his eye when he asked."

"I definitely think he's interested."

"I told him we'd have to have another get together, so maybe after we get back from LA, we can plan something, like a cookout."

"Sounds like a plan. Wanna go sit under the willow tree?"

"Sure."

We get up and Damien holds my hand as we walk together. We both sit down, and he wraps his arms around, laying me down in the grass. He crushes his lips to mine. I can feel his desire the way his tongue is exploring my mouth. My heart races as I return his passionate kiss. If we weren't outside in broad daylight, I'd already be pulling his clothes off. He doesn't seem to care, as I feel his hands under my shirt. Fuck, I want this.

"We can't do this here! Someone will see."

"Fine, but one night, we are going to. For now, get that sweet little ass in bed. NOW!"

"Make me," I say, sticking out my tongue at him.

Damien starts tickling me until I can't breathe. I get up and try to run away, but he catches me and puts me over his shoulder. He calls the dogs in and carries me into the house. He doesn't put me down until we're in our bedroom. He narrows his eyes at me, hands on his hips.

"You're in trouble now, woman. I'm going to make that sweet pussy come over and over until you're screaming for me to stop."

"No fuckin' way will I ask you to stop. I can take anything that tongue can dish out."

"Well, Miss Sassy-mouth, we'll see about that. Get naked and lie on the bed."

I do as I'm told. Damien stands at the foot of the bed, licking his sexy lips. I'm so wet and horny for him, I can barely stand it.

"Good girl. Spread those legs. I need to see that hot pussy."

I feel a little self-conscious, but one look at my sexy man melts that away. Never removing his eyes from me, he starts removing his clothes and I just about pass out. He's so damn hot!

"Get those fingers and spread that sweet pussy wide. Good. Now, tease that clit for me, babe."

As my cheeks redden, I start stroking my clit. My jaw drops when I see Damien grab his dick and start pumping. The thought of him getting himself off from watching me do the same nearly sends me over the edge. He suddenly stops and climbs onto the bed. His head makes its way between my legs and he sucks my clit hard. Holy fucking shit! He switches to his tongue, licking hard and fast. I feel him slip a couple of fingers inside me, sliding them in and out.

"Fuck, so good. Oh, Damien."

"You taste delicious, babe. I can't get enough."

He gets back to sucking me like a peach and my body quivers. He feels it and sucks harder. I come undone with a vengeance, writhing beneath him. His mouth doesn't leave my pussy, sucking even as I come hard. He slides his hands under my ass and lifts my hips off the bed, squeezing my ass as his mouth continues its sweet assault between my legs. I come over and over, each orgasm arriving faster than the one before. My entire body convulses as I scream his name. Still, he doesn't stop, and the pleasure is almost too much to bear. But I'm determined not to let him win. I will not do what he wants me to! Suddenly, he stops and gets off the bed.

"Finally had enough of me?" I say.

"Smug, are we? I'm not even close to having enough. Time to up the game, though."

My mouth opens, but no words come out. What else could he possibly do to me and how am I going to handle it? I watch him walk to the dresser and open the top drawer. Oh, shit! He walks back to the bed with one of our toys and I know I'm in trouble now. He also has a blindfold with him. Fuck! He puts the blindfold on me, so I can no longer see where he is. I feel the bed move when he climbs in. I know he's close; I can feel his warm breath on my stomach. I feel him back between my legs. I hear the quiet buzz of the vibrator and brace myself.

I gasp as he slides Bob's full length inside me and turns the pulse to maximum power. He leaves it inside me, pulsing hard at my g-spot. I hear another buzzing sound and feel strong vibrations on my clit. My body bucks off the bed. I don't know how much longer I can hang on, but I'm determined. I come hard and fast, the vibrations driving my already sensitive clit crazy. Meanwhile, the pulsing inside me makes me squirt hard. Damien growls as he watches me explode. Still, I will not ask him to stop. There's no way his cock can hold out much longer. After a couple more strong orgasms, including one more drenching squirt, he turns both toys off.

"Fuck. Babe. You win. I need my dick inside you. Don't move."

I couldn't even if I wanted to. My legs feel like jelly and I'm still quivering. He removes the blindfold and tosses it aside. He kisses me hard and I can taste myself on his mouth. I feel his cock enter me hard, taking my breath away. He's harder than I've ever felt him, which I didn't even know was possible. He fucks me hard and fast, filling me with his hot come. He stays inside me, holding me tight against him, kissing me with an intense passion. I feel him harden and he fucks me again. After a second load spills inside me, he moves next to me and pulls me close.

"Babe. You're the queen and I bow to you. No woman has even come close to handling what you just did."

"And don't you ever forget it," I say as I smile widely.

Chapter Ten

Damien

"Babe, while you're finishing up, I'm going to take the dogs over to Judd's house."

"Okay, one second."

Lexi comes out of the bedroom. She crouches down and gives both dogs some love.

"Be good for Uncle Judd," she says, using baby talk, and my dick stirs.

There isn't a damn thing my woman does that fails to get me horny. If we weren't getting ready to head to the airport, I'd be pounding that hot pussy. Fuck, I gotta stay focused. Lexi finishes her goodbyes and heads back into the bedroom. I load the dogs and their stuff in my car and drive over to Judd's farm. I see him sitting on the porch, waiting. He walks down when I finish parking.

I let the dogs out of the car, then grab their stuff. Judd helps me take everything inside. I hand him an envelope.

"Lexi wrote out detailed instructions for you. You know women!"

"No worries. I want to do things exactly the way you both do."

"I really appreciate this. She included Melissa's phone number in case you need any help."

"Sounds good. The dogs will be well taken care of, so you two just focus on what you need to. I know this has to be rough."

"It is. I'm more grateful than ever that Lexi will be by my side." I smile slightly.

"She's a good woman."

I nod, thoughts of that woman, MY woman, filling my head.

"Okay, Dave and Maggie, behave. We'll be home in a few days."

"Safe travels."

"Thanks again for everything."

I head back home and see the luggage on the porch. I smile. That woman never ceases to amaze me. I spent way too many years dealing with spoiled brats who expected you to do everything for them. Then I meet this woman. Miss Independent Sassypants. And she knows how to give one hell of a hot blow job! I see Lexi come outside and it takes every bit of my self-control not to ravage her.

"Are you ready to go, babe?"

"All set. I just need to lock up."

The limo I ordered pulls into the driveway. We carry our luggage to the car and make our way to Philly International. I booked first-class tickets for this trip since flights to LA are usually packed. I'm having a hard time with the thought of Jack being gone, and the last thing I feel like dealing with is a crowd. I just want to be snuggled in a seat next to my woman.

When we arrive, the driver drops us at the Delta terminal. We make our way through security and to the first-class lounge to wait for our flight to board. They call us to board, so Lexi and I head down the tunnel and find our seats. While we wait for the coach passengers to board, a flight attendant takes our drink and food order. We each order a screwdriver and a sandwich. Once we're in the air, the attendants serve our food and drinks. After we're done, Lexi lays her head on my shoulder and falls asleep. A little while later, she stirs and lifts her head.

"I'm sorry."

"No need to be. I love when you do that."

"Really?"

"Babe, you're my world. I love you."

She looks up at me, eyes damp, and whispers, "I love you so much."

We sit together quietly, holding hands, for the rest of the flight. The flight attendants come around and collect all the trash and glasses. We hear the pilot announce to begin preparation for descent, so we buckle our seatbelts and wait. As we touch down, a fresh wave of despair washes over me, so I grab Lexi's hand. She squeezes mine tight, and I know she understands.

We disembark, get our luggage, then head to the rental car lot. All I want right now is to lie with Lexi in my arms, so I drive us right to the hotel. Once we're in the room, we both take off our shoes, climb into bed, and take a much-needed nap. We wake up famished. Since our bodies are on East Coast time, it's far too early to go out for dinner, so we just order some room service. After we're done eating, we decide to take a relaxing dip in the soaking tub in our bathroom. I'm feeling more relaxed than I have all day. I'm also feeling something else, sitting here naked with my woman.

"Babe, I really need to be inside you. I just need to forget why we're here for a little while."

Without a word, she gets out of the tub and dries off. When she's done, she walks over to the bed and wags her finger at me. I dry off and join her. She climbs on top and takes my entire length inside her sweet pussy. She rocks her hips, sliding my cock in and out of her. Fuck, she feels so good.

"Harder, babe."

She locks her eyes with mine and increases her pace. She remains quiet as she bounces hard. I lose myself in her. My only focus is on my cock inside her wetness. I move my hands to her hot little ass and squeeze hard as she fucks me. She lets me take what I need from her until I lose control and fill her with a huge load. I roll her onto her back, my dick still buried deep inside her. I lift her hips off the bed to get a better angle and thrust hard. She moans softly as we fuck. Her body quivers as she explodes, but still she stays quiet. She lets me fuck her over and over until I have nothing left. I lay next to her and pull her close.

"Thank you, babe."

"My pleasure."

This woman, so selfless in her love for me, is the reason I get out of bed in the morning. She's mine and mine alone. Nobody will ever change that, and nobody will ever hurt her. She yawns into my chest. I pull the covers up, turn off the light next to the bed, and kiss her hard.

"Good night, babe."

"Good night, my love."

Chapter Eleven

Lexi

I wake up the next morning and move to the other side of the bed. Damien isn't there. I hear a guitar quietly strumming, so I walk out to the living area of our suite. Damien's sitting there naked except for his guitar. My mouth waters. I sit down on the couch and just listen. There's something so sad about the song he's playing, understandable with what we have to do today.

"What time are we meeting up with Billy?"

"He said 10. I thought we could run downstairs for a quick breakfast before we head out."

"I'm definitely hungry after last night."

"I'm sorry about that."

"What do you mean?"

"I was selfish."

"Again, what do you mean?"

"I can't explain it."

"Let me try. I can't imagine how hard this is for you. When you told me you needed me to help you forget, that's what I tried to do. I wanted to give you what you needed, so I let you take it. But please, I certainly enjoyed it. What you did to me, particularly between my legs, was unlike anything I've ever experienced." I reassure him.

"Thank you."

"My pleasure! Now, how about we go clean ourselves up and feed a different appetite?"

"What would I do without you?"

"You'd be fine, but you'll never have to find out. You're stuck with me."

He leans in and kisses me. My heart nearly leaps out of my chest. He gets up and walks to the bedroom, giving me a pleasant view of that perfectly sculpted ass. After a hot, steamy shower, we get dressed and go down to the hotel restaurant. After breakfast, the valet brings our rental around, and we drive to the funeral home. Billy asked us to meet him here to go over the final arrangements for Jack's service. I see a man standing outside when we pull into the parking lot.

"That's Billy," Damien says.

"He looks so sad. My heart goes out to him."

"Mine too."

I give Damien's hand a light squeeze before we get out of the car. He takes my hand as we approach Billy.

"Good morning, Billy. This is my girlfriend, Lexi."

"Pleasure to meet you," Billy said.

"I wish it were under better circumstances. I'm so very sorry for your loss."

"Thank you. Let's head inside."

The three of us walk in together. The funeral director, Steven, greets us each with a handshake.

"Shall we go to my office?" Steven said.

"Yes, lets," Billy answered.

"I can wait out here, if you prefer," I said, unsure what to do since I didn't know Jack personally.

Damien nods yes, so I take a seat in the lobby. I see Steven send a quick text and a few minutes later, a younger version of him appears.

"Hello, ma'am. I'm Steven's son, Kyle. He asked me to see if you needed anything while you wait? We have a small kitchen area with some light refreshments and a TV, if you'd like."

"Thank you, that would be great."

I follow Kyle to the kitchen, grab a cup of coffee, and sit down. I grab my phone and text Melissa.

"How are things there?"

"All good. Saw dogs yesterday."

"Hmmmm...."

"It's not what you think."

"Riiiight."

"They were at the park, so I stopped."

"Mmm hmm..."

"Stop it, bitch!"

"Hussie. You know you want to ride that."

"LEXI!"

"I know you, girl."

"How are things there?"

"Fine, change the subject, but this isn't over. Damien is struggling a bit, but to be expected."

"Send him my love. Gotta run, meeting starting."

"See you when we get home."

"Laters."

I'm more determined than ever to get those two together. No time to focus on that now, but when we get home, it's operation "Ride a Cowboy." I bring up the Kindle app on my phone and start reading a book by another of my favorite authors, JJ Grice. I'll never turn down a good romance novel! I get so engrossed in the story, I don't notice Damien and Billy standing there. Damien clears his throat and I drop my phone.

"I'm sorry, babe," Damien says, laughing.

"You know me when it comes to reading."

"I sure do."

"I think you better apologize," Billy says with a smile.

"It's okay," I reply.

"I'd love to treat you both to lunch."

"We'd love to have lunch, but you don't need to pay," Damien says.

"I want to. It means the world to me you came all this way."

"Well, we appreciate it. Thank you," I say.

We walk out to the parking lot together. Billy tells Damien to follow him. Billy pulls into the parking lot of a Chinese restaurant and parks. We take the spot next to him and the three of us enter the restaurant together. The seating host knows Billy, so he takes us to a special table where we're waited on right away. After we order, Damien and Billy share stories about Jack.

It warms my heart hearing how much Damien loved and respected his mentor. Not to mention the beautiful romance between Jack and Billy. I'm grateful Jack came into Damien's life. I can't imagine how his life would have differed without the positive influence Jack had on his life. I think about Damien's past, at least what he's revealed. I can't help but wonder if he'll run into anyone at the service tomorrow.

The waiter brings our drinks. Billy holds up his glass. Damien and I join him.

"A toast to my one and only love. I'll never forget you, Jack."

"To Jack," Damien and I say in unison.

Once our food comes, we all sit and eat quietly. Looking back and forth between Billy and Damien, my heart hurts. Tomorrow is going to be hell. I hope Billy has someone there for moral support. After we finish lunch, Billy pays the check and we all head outside.

"Thank you both again for making the trip out here. It means the world to me. I'll see you both in the morning. I need to get home and get some rest before tomorrow."

Damien doesn't respond, and I can see he's struggling.

"We understand. Please take care of yourself tonight. We'll see you tomorrow," I respond.

I give Billy a hug before he gets in his car and drives home. Damien pulls me close and I feel tears soaking the shoulder of my t-shirt. I hold him as tight as I can. His body shakes as the tears flow. He collapses to the ground. I sit next to him and wrap my arms around him. He sobs loudly, holding on to me for dear life. My heart shatters for him and at the same time, I've never loved him more. We sit like this for over an hour.

Chapter Twelve

Damien

I can't believe I just lost it like that. Lexi must think I'm a wuss. I can't bring myself to even look at her.

"I'm sorry. I understand if it's over," I say quietly.

"Over? Why would you think that?"

"My pathetic display. Real men don't act like that."

"Who told you that?"

"My dad."

"You listen to me, Damien St. James! Anyone who thinks a man showing his emotions makes him less of a man is an ass. Now, let me tell you the truth. I already love you more than I ever knew was possible. But, just now, holding you while you released everything I know you've been holding inside, I realized that I could love you more. And now, I do."

"Really?"

"You've given me the gift of confidence and self-worth, something I thought I'd never find. What I can give you back is the compassion and support your father never did. You are a real man and I will never let you forget it."

"Babe, thank you. I love you so much. I think we've sat here long enough."

"I agree. My ass is starting to hurt."

I get up and help Lexi up. I look at her and my heart swells. This woman, and what she's done for me. She has no idea the extent to which she's saved me. I intend to spend the rest of my life showing her. When we get back home, it's time to put "operation marriage proposal" into action. I have some ideas about where I want to send her hunting for clues. I can't wait.

We head back to the hotel and I point some sights out to Lexi on the way. If we had more time, I would love to show her some of my old hangouts. But that isn't why we're here. That feeling of sadness washes over me again. I feel a squeeze on my hand. I glance over and Lexi is watching me. No woman has ever gotten me, but somehow, this beauty does. It still blows my hand how her ex could just throw her away. Dumbass. Once we're back at the hotel, we ride the elevator in silence.

"How about another relaxing soak in the tub," Lexi says when we're back in the room.

"Sitting naked with you in a tub sounds perfect."

Lexi smiles at me and does this little shake of her hips and ass. I lick my lips and feel my dick stirring. Fuck, those curves drive me wild. I don't think I'll ever get enough of that body. That hot, sexy, soft body. And damn, does she know how to work it, how to please me. She's mine and mine alone. While Lexi's getting the tub ready, I order some champagne and strawberries.

"Does that mean we're playing the hooker and the millionaire tonight?"

"Nah, Julia Roberts has nothing on you, babe. I just wanna play with my Lexi."

"Mmmm, I like the sound of that."

Once our room service arrives, I put everything near the tub and we climb in. Lexi turns the jets on full blast. The warm water and powerful jets immediately relax all the tension in my body. I pour us each a glass of champagne. After a quick toast, we each take a sip and enjoy a strawberry. Lexi nestles her body against mine and boom, I'm hard as a rock. I feel her soft hand wrap around my dick and stroke me gently. A deep groan escapes my lips. She doesn't stop until her hand is covered with my seed. I sigh, feeling even more relaxed. Now, it's her turn.

"Spread those sexy legs."

I slide a couple of fingers inside her, teasing her clit with my thumb. She's so wet for me. I fuck her hard with my fingers until I feel her body quiver. She explodes around me with a loud moan as I stroke her swollen clit. I need to get her into that bed now.

"Woman, get that hot little ass out of this tub and onto the bed. NOW."

She quickly climbs out and dries herself off. I notice a little extra sway in those sexy hips as she prances off to the bedroom. I climb out, dry off, grab the strawberries, and follow her. Her eyes go wide when she sees me carrying the plate of strawberries. She looks like a goddess lying there naked. I grab a strawberry then lay down next to her. I drag it down between her sexy tits and down her body.

"Open those legs for me, babe."

She spreads her legs as wide as she can, giving me a full view of her soaking wet pussy. I swipe the strawberry up her folds and tease her clit with it. She moans, but no words come out. I tease her again with the strawberry. Not breaking eye contact with her, I pop it into my mouth.

"Delicious, baby. I need more."

I bury my head between her silky thighs and swipe my tongue up and down her pussy. I turn my focus to her clit, not stopping my assault until her body explodes. I slide up her body and thrust my dick deep inside her. I fuck her slowly, giving her the full length of my cock with each thrust, while her hands explore my body. Listening to her sweet moans send me over the edge and I fill her.

"Get on your back, Damien."

I do as I'm told, watching as she grabs a strawberry and swirls the head of my cock with it. She licks it, then pops in her mouth. Damn, that woman is sexy as hell. She gets on all fours and wraps her mouth around my cock. She takes my entire length down her throat. Each stroke of those sexy full lips sends jolts of electricity through my body.

She stops before I come and mounts me. I love watching my woman fuck me.

She leans back and grabs my legs for support as her hot curves bounce on my dick. I tease her clit with a couple of fingers while she's fucking me. She unleashes a string of the dirtiest words I've ever heard as her entire body convulses. I can't hold back and I fill her with another load. She collapses down on my chest, her body glistening with sweat. I gently roll her onto her back, holding her tight. There's nothing hotter than a woman who knows exactly what her man needs. She lets out a huge yawn.

"Tired, babe?"

"Mmmm, thanks to my sexy stud. Fuck, that was incredible."

"Oh, babe. It was mind-blowing."

She smiles at me and my heart swells. We get ready for bed, then climb under the covers. Lexi lies on her side and quickly falls asleep. I spoon her, holding my babe tight. It's the last thing I remember until the sun awakens us the next morning.

Chapter Thirteen

Lexi

I wake up in the morning, still wrapped in Damien's arms. I kiss him on his cheek.

"Do you want some breakfast, baby?"

"I'm not sure I can eat, babe."

"I understand, but you should. Let me order some room service."

"Okay, babe, you know what I like."

I smile, my mind going right to the dirty place. I order each of us a breakfast platter. Damien has moved from the bed to the couch, so I sit down next to him. I lay my head on his shoulder. All I want to do today is comfort him and be there for him. He tousles my hair.

"Thanks, babe."

"For what?"

"Always knowing what I need."

"That's what I'm here for."

We hear a knock on the door. I grab the room service tray and carry it over to the little dining table. After we finish eating, Damien puts the tray out in the hallway. I can see the sadness in his eyes today and it hurts my heart. I hope he can get through today.

"I'm going to grab a shower," Damien says.

"I'll join you."

"Babe, I love showering together, but just for today, I need some time alone."

"I understand."

While Damien's in the shower, I sit on the couch. I miss showering with him, but I understand why needs this time by himself. I pick up his guitar and start strumming. I've never played before, so I have no idea what I'm doing. I got so focused on it I didn't hear him come out of the bathroom.

"Babe, I didn't know you could play."

"I can't."

"The hell you can't. That sounded fantastic."

"I've never even picked up a guitar before."

"Damn, woman, you're a natural. If you want to learn more, I'll teach you."

"I'd love to."

Damien flashes me that smile that melts my heart. It's the first time I've seen it since we got to California. I put the guitar down for now, though, as I need to get showered. Once I'm done, I put on a simple black dress and a pair of black flats. Damien looks handsome in his suit, though I wish he was wearing it for any other reason. He calls the front desk to have his car brought around and we head downstairs to wait.

"Babe, do you mind driving today? Having a hard time focusing."

"Sure. You just need to tell me where to go."

"Thanks."

Damien directs me to the funeral home. Billy is waiting and points to the space next to his car. I park and we cross the parking lot. I walk behind Billy and Damien. They walk in and Steven greets them. He goes over the schedule with them, then walks us to the door of the room. He opens the door, but Billy and Damien don't walk in.

"Are you ready to do this?" Billy says.

"As ready as I'll ever be," Damien says.

I wait outside, giving them time to pay their respects to Jack. A little while later, Damien joins me in the lobby, his eyes moist. He pulls me in tight, as if his life depended on it. I hug him with every ounce of strength I have, trying to bring him some peace.

"Are you ready to go back in?" I ask him.

"Only with you by my side."

He holds my hand as we walk inside. Billy is standing next to the casket, so I walk over and give him a hug.

"Thank you for being here for Damien."

"Of course. I'm here for you too, if I can do anything."

"You just did. Thank you. Would you mind if Damien stands up here with me? Jack always said Damien was like the son he never had."

"I don't mind at all."

"Thanks. Please have a seat in the front row, and we'll join you once the receiving line is done."

I take a seat and watch as Billy asks Damien to stand up front with him. As we approach the time the doors open for the public, I hear a buzz in the lobby. I turn and see a long line of mourners already. I notice that a lot of them are high school age. I've always held educators in high regard, especially the way they helped me throughout my challenging school years. Jack's students felt that way about him.

Steven walks over and tells Billy that they are going to open the doors. Billy nods and looks at Damien, who also nods. Steven walks to the back and lets mourners enter the room. Billy introduces Damien to each group as they come through. Everyone has the same sad look on their face as they pass by the casket. Jack was one of those special people and I wish I'd had the chance to meet him. Damien's face always brightens when he tells me stories.

I look over and Billy seems to get faint, so I walk out to the lobby and ask for two bottles of water. I also grab them each a cookie. I interrupt the line for a moment to hand them each a water and a cookie. They each wolf down their cookie and water. Billy looks better, so I move and let the receiving line continue to filter through. The seats behind us are filling up, so the staff sets up more rows of chairs.

After a couple of hours, the line shortens. Billy and Damien look exhausted, and there's still a lot of the day left. I grab them each a cup of coffee and another cookie. I feel so helpless. All I want to do is take their pain away and I can't. The coffee does the trick and they both perk up a bit. Damien's former bandmates come in. He tells them who I am, so they stop by and chat with me for a couple of minutes before they find a seat.

There's a break in people coming through, so they both take a chance to sit down for a few minutes.

"Do either of you need anything?" I ask.

"We're good, babe," Damien says.

"Yes, thanks for everything you did this morning," Billy says.

"No problem at all. Just wave if you need something."

I walk back to my seat. It's getting close to the end of the reception portion and the line is dwindling down. I see one latecomer, a man, approaching the line. Damien looks over and his entire body tenses up. I take a closer look. The man reminds me of Damien, only older. Holy shit, it couldn't be.

"What the hell are you doing here, Dad?" I hear Damien say.

Chapter Fourteen

Damien

I can't believe he had the goddamn nerve to show his fucking face here. I look over at Lexi and I can see the concern in her eyes. The last thing I wanted was for her to have to see the man who almost ruined me. I know how hard it was for Lexi to hear me talk about bullying other kids after what she went through. But instead of judging me, that amazing woman wrapped her arms around me and held me tight. I won't let the king of the assholes do anything to jeopardize what we have.

"I asked you a question," I say. I'm trying to hold my anger inside.

"Is that any way to talk to your father?"

"I won't hash this out here."

"Fine, I have all day. I cleared my schedule to be here."

"Whatever."

It was time for the memorial service to start, so Billy and I sat down next to Lexi. She took my hand in hers, and I calmed down. She has this amazing way of making me feel better. The pastor from Billy and Jack's church comes up to the podium. After a brief eulogy and sermon, he invites anyone who has a story to come up front and share. Billy went up first and told the story of how he and Jack met. I heard Lexi sniffle. I looked over and tears were streaming down her face.

"I want to go up, but I need you standing with me."

She nods and squeezes my hand, so I stand. She joins me and we walk up to the podium. I talk about the first time I met Jack and how he helped me. I never would have made it through that without Lexi next to me. She has no idea just how much she's my rock. I never thought I'd depend on a woman, but she truly makes me a better man. We sit back down and listen as several more people come up front and tell stories.

"It's obvious how special Jack was," Lexi says.

"He was the best," I reply.

Once the service is done, they invite the mourners to pay their final respects. Several of Jack's students are acting as pallbearers, so they stay behind with Billy, Lexi and I. Steven waits for Lexi and me, then Billy to say our last goodbyes, then closes the casket. He instructs the pall bearers on how to carry the casket. Once they have it secured, we all start the walk out to the parking lot. Billy's legs are shaking, so Lexi holds onto him and helps him walk outside. My amazing rock.

Lexi helps Billy get into the limo, then grabs our rental. Steven holds up the procession so she can get in line behind the limo. I jump in the passenger seat. She grabs my hand while we wait for the rest of the cars to get lined up. I hope I make it through the rest of today. I'm especially on edge after seeing my asshole father and I'm dreading having to confront him later.

One of Steven's staff puts on an orange vest and stops traffic so the procession can start the drive to the cemetery. I turn the radio on, hoping some music will help me calm down. It only helps a little, though. What calms me most is watching Lexi. I love the way her brow wrinkles up when she's concentrating. I let my eyes wander down her body and my mind follows. I head right to the naughtiest of places, bringing me that sense of calm I needed. We stop at a red light and she looks over at me.

"What is that look on your face?"

"I was thinking about being naked with you. I know it may not seem the most appropriate time, but sex with you calms me. Thinking about it is helping me, especially after having the added distress of him showing up today."

"I'm flattered that you think I'm that powerful."

"You are, my beautiful goddess. I love you."

"I love you, too."

The light changes, so we move once the limo does. The rest of the ride to the cemetery goes smoothly. We pull in and park behind the limo. We walk over to the car and join Billy. Once the pallbearers have assembled, Lexi links arms with both Billy and me and the three of us walk behind the casket. For the thousandth time today, I'm beyond grateful for this amazing woman. We sit down in the three front chairs and wait for the rest of the mourners to join us. The pastor runs through a small ceremony. The funeral home staff hands each of us a sunflower, Jack's favorite.

Billy goes up first, lays his flower down, and collapses forward onto the casket. Lexi and I walk up and lay our flowers next. She takes Billy's arm and helps him back to this chair, then rejoins me. She takes my hand as I whisper one last goodbye, then return to our chairs. We sit and watch the blur of people walking through to place their flowers. As everyone's walking by, Steven announces the location of the luncheon and asks people to let him know if they're attending, so he can provide an approximate headcount to the banquet hall.

Once everyone has gone back to their cars, Steven comes over to us to let us know he took care of things with the owner of the hall. Billy, Lexi, and I get up and head to the cars. The funeral staff heads out and Billy realizes the limo won't be going to the luncheon.

"I wasn't thinking about that," Billy says.

"No worries, we have plenty of room," Lexi says.

"You've already done more than enough for me today."

"Nonsense, it's my pleasure."

I watch Lexi grab his arm and walk him to our car. I climb in the back and Billy rides up front with Lexi, so he can direct her to the banquet hall. We walk inside together and I tense up when I see my father. Fucker. I try to ignore him, but as the luncheon is winding down, he corners me.

"Can't you just leave me alone?"

"No, you need to hear me out."

"The hell I do."

"I'm your father."

"No, you were mom's sperm donor."

He nods toward Lexi. "Who's the hussie?"

"Don't you dare call her that. She's the most incredible woman I've ever known."

"She'll leave when she finds out what you were like."

"I told her everything."

"And she stayed?"

I'm about to answer when I hear Lexi's voice and damn, is she angry.

"Not only did I stay, but it made me love him even more. How Jack helped him find the right path and become a better version of himself is incredible."

"Whatever. You jackasses deserve each other."

"That's the first thing you've ever said that I've agreed with. And now that I've said my peace, I finally have the closure I needed. I will leave you with one last thought. GO ROT IN HELL."

I turn and walk away before he can respond, Billy and Lexi hot on my heels. We get to the car, and all I want to do is get the hell out of here. Not just here, but I can't wait to fly back home tomorrow. We drive Billy home and say our goodbyes. We promise to keep in touch. After we see he's inside, we drive back to the hotel.

Chapter Fifteen

Lexi

Damien said little on the way back to the hotel. I can't imagine with everything that happened today, he's able to process anything. When we're in the room, he sits down on the couch, his head in his hands. I sit down next to him and lay my head on his shoulder.

"I'm here if you want to talk."

"Thanks, babe."

After a few minutes, he gets up and walks to the bedroom. I don't follow until I hear him call my name. I walk in and he's getting ready for bed. I get into my jammies as well. After we both finish our nightly routines, we climb into bed. Damien grabs the remote and turns the TV on.

"I really just need to sit and relax. I hope that's okay."

"Anything you need, baby."

"I have exactly what I need sitting next to me. I love you, babe."

"I love you, too."

We watch a couple reruns of Impractical Jokers, always a mood booster since it's so damn hilarious. Damien puts his arm around my shoulders, so I nestle in close. I hear him sigh. I'm relieved he's feeling a little calmer.

"Babe."

"What's up?"

"I hated fucking seeing my father today. He's lucky I didn't break his fucking nose when he called you a hussie." He seethes.

"I know. Just know that I was able to brush it off. He doesn't know me."

"And he never will. I said the things I've been wanting to say all these years. I can now put him behind me."

"Glad to hear it. Now, how are you otherwise? I can only imagine how hard laying Jack to rest was."

"It was, but my concern is Billy."

"I love that about you, but I'm also concerned about you."

"No judgement, please, babe."

"Never."

"It was the hardest fucking thing I've ever had to do. So many times, I wanted to run out of the room."

"But you didn't."

"That's because of you. Every time I thought about running, I looked over at you. You may not even realize, but you've been my rock today. I never would have gotten through it without you."

I watch as tears spill over and Damien sobs. My heart breaks for him. I turn and wrap my arms around him, holding him as tight as I can. He pulls me tight against him. Neither of us moves, we just lie there holding each other. His sobs finally subside and he loosens his grip a little.

"I'm sorry, babe."

"For what?"

"Losing it."

"You didn't lose it. You dealt with your grief in a very healthy way. Men need to stop being afraid to show their emotions. I get why you are. I've seen the way guys treat each other, but this woman does not think any less of you." I reassure him.

"Thank you for never making me feel any less of a man."

"Because you aren't. Trust me, you are one hundred percent a real man."

"Oh, is that so? I would love to show you, but I'm exhausted. I do have a favor to ask and I hope you don't find this weird."

"I'm queen of the weirdos, so I think you'll be fine."

"Nothing comforts me more than feeling your skin against mine. I want to get naked and just hold you while we watch TV."

"Mmmm, that sounds divine."

We both get out of our jammies and back in bed. Damien pulls the covers up, then pulls me close. As we're flipping channels, I see one of my all-time favorite movies, Flashdance.

"I love that movie."

"Then Flashdance it is, babe."

The next thing we know, it's morning, and the TV is still going. We need to get up and get moving as we are flying home today. We grab a quick shower and get dressed. Damien checks out on his phone while I get our luggage together. We head downstairs and wait for our rental car. After we return that, we head inside and get in the security line.

Once we've gotten through security, we walk to the first class lounge and grab a quick bite to hold us over until we're in the air. When they call us to board, we head down the tunnel, both of us relieved to be heading home. I miss the dogs and the comfort of the familiar. I could never have been a rockstar like Damien. I get nervous in unfamiliar surroundings, though it wasn't as bad this time. I think my mind was preoccupied with taking care of Damien and helping Billy.

Several hours later, we touch down in my favorite city. We grab our luggage then take the shuttle to the long term parking lot to grab Damien's car. I smile when we're finally sitting in his driveway. We put the luggage in the house and walk out back. Both dogs are outside in Judd's yard. Maggie sees us first and starts wiggling from head to tail. She lets out a loud bark. That gets Dave's attention and we're greeted by synchronized butt wiggles and excited squeaks. Judd loads both dogs onto his tractor.

"I'll be right over with the kiddos."

We hear the tractor pull into the driveway and we see two flashes of fur run into the backyard. Damien and Judd walk over to the table and sit down.

"Can I get anyone something to drink?" I ask.

"Iced tea, ma'am, if it's not too much trouble," Judd said.

"Same for me, please, babe."

"No trouble at all."

I return a few minutes later carrying a tray with a pitcher of iced tea and three glasses. After pouring everyone a glass, I sit down with the guys.

"Welcome home, you two. The dogs were great, but they definitely missed you."

"Thank you again for being willing to watch them," Damien said.

"Yes, thank you," I add.

"My pleasure. Miss Melissa stopped by a couple of times to check on them."

I swear I saw Judd blush when he said Melissa's name. I plan on pumping her for details later. I catch Damien's eye and I see him trying to hide a smile. I can't help but wonder what else Melissa checked on while she was there. Judd and Damien chat about how things went, so I go out to the yard to play with the dogs for a bit. I grab a couple of tennis balls from their toy bucket and within seconds, they're both zooming around the yard. I look over at Damien and think to myself how much I love my life. I run with the dogs as they head toward the willow tree in the back corner of the yard.

Chapter Sixteen

Damien

I watch Lexi out in the yard playing with Maggie and Dave, and my heart swells. I've found the life, and the woman, I've always wanted. I see them run to the far corner of the yard, so I know she's out of earshot.

"I'm going to need some help from you and Melissa. I'm working on the final touches for a very special scavenger hunt."

"Scavenger hunt?"

"Yeah, I'm creating a few riddles that will send Lexi around town and bring her to the dog park. I'll be waiting there with the dogs to propose to her."

"Congratulations, man. I'm honored to help. What do you need me to do?" He asks.

"I'm going to need some help to set up the riddles."

"I'd love to. Where are you planning to send her?"

"I'm going to start with the club, then Palermo's pizza. From there, Harvest Moon Bed and Breakfast and the dog park. Each riddle will direct her to the next place."

"I love that idea. I know she will too."

"Thanks. I would also like for you and Melissa to be there and help with pictures and video." I ask.

"Of course. Can I ask you something?"

"Shoot."

"Is Melissa seeing anyone?"

"No, she's not."

"Oh. I wonder why."

"I'm not sure. Are you interested?"

"I think she's pretty, but I just couldn't."

"Why not, man?"

"Forget I said anything."

"Got it. Are you sure you're still okay helping with the proposal?"

"Yes, but hush for now. Lexi's headed this way."

"Thanks, man."

"I gotta run. The farm awaits."

"Thank you again for taking care of the dogs," Lexi says.

Judd tips his hat, then gets on his tractor and heads back to his farm. As soon as he's gone, I tell Lexi about the strange conversation I had with him.

"I've been wondering if he had someone hurt him. Might explain why he won't pursue things with Mel. It makes me sad, though, as I can tell she likes him too."

"I see your wheels spinning."

"They are not." She disagrees.

"Babe. I know what you're thinking, and it's not a good idea."

"But they belong together."

"I know you think so, and honestly, I agree. It's not our place, though. We need to let them figure it out for themselves."

"But what if they don't?"

"Then it wasn't meant to be."

Lexi sighs, then suddenly starts laughing hysterically.

"Why are you looking at me like I just lost my damn mind?"

"Dare I ask, babe?"

"I started thinking of an old Kenny Chesney song. I pictured Judd singing it to Mel."

"What song?"

"She Thinks My Tractor's Sexy."

"I don't think I've heard that one."

"Hang on."

Lexi brings up the song on YouTube and plays it for me. By the end, we're both having trouble breathing from laughing so hard. We spend the rest of the night chilling on the couch, exhausted from our day of travel. The next morning, we're lying in bed.

"I want to fix Mel and Judd up."

"What am I going to do with you, babe?" I sigh.

"I can think of a few things."

"Let me guess, they all involve us being naked."

"You know me too well."

"You certainly aren't the woman I first met."

"Is that good or bad?"

"Depends on your perspective."

"And what's yours?"

"Get up and I'll tell you."

She stands and I walk over to her, throw her over my shoulder, and carry her out of the bedroom. I put her down in the living room.

"Your ass. Naked and on that couch. NOW," she says.

I do as I'm told and watch as Lexi does a sexy striptease for me. Two seconds in and I was hard. By the time she was done, I had to fight not to grab my cock. I want this woman so fucking bad. She's completely naked now. Her hands travel the length of her body, stopping at my favorite part. I watch her tease herself with a finger and I just about blow my load. My jaw drops and a smile spreads across her face.

"See something you like?" she says.

"Fuck yeah, babe."

She climbs into my lap, her pussy taking the full length of my dick inside her. Fuck, she feels incredible. I wrap my arms around her and pull her close to me. She bounces all those delicious curves up and down my cock as suck on her sexy tits. All I need now is some dirty talk from those beautiful lips.

As if on cue, I hear her say, "Oh fuck, your fucking cock feels so good inside me. I love the way you stretch my pussy."

"Fuck, my naughty woman."

"Mmmm. And what do naughty girls deserve?"

"What, babe?"

"A spanking. Please let me feel your hands on my ass."

I give her a light swat on her sexy little ass and she bounces harder. I love how turned on these get her and I swat again, a little harder this time.

"Oh, yes, Damien. Feels so fucking good."

I move one hand around and stroke her clit with my thumb. I watch her chest heaving as her moans get louder. I can feel how close she is, but I want this to last.

"Babe, get that hot ass on the couch."

She climbs off and sits down.

"Spread those legs for me. Wide."

She opens as far as she can and my eyes go right to her soaking wet pussy.

"Good girl."

I kneel in front of her, lightly swiping her folds with my tongue. She throws her head back and moans. I continue teasing her with light, slow licks. I feel her hands in my hair. I know I'm driving her crazy, so I increase the pressure.

"Fuck, so good. Please let me come, Damien."

"I'm not convinced I should."

"What do I have to do?"

"Beg."

"Damien, please, baby. My pussy's throbbing. I need to come now. Please."

"And what will you do for me if I let you come?"

"Anything you want."

"Good answer. If I let you come, I want you on your knees on that couch. I'm going to fuck your pussy from behind while I spank that naughty ass."

"Oh, Damien. I want that."

I suck her clit hard and slide a couple of fingers inside her. In no time at all, she explodes. Her body quakes as she screams. As soon as she's done, I watch her stand, turn, and kneel on the couch. I thrust my dick into her and pound her sweet pussy hard. I give her a light swat on her ass. It doesn't take me long and I empty myself inside her.

We're sitting on the couch kissing when we hear a call pull in the driveway. We hear Mel's voice, so we both scramble to get dressed. Lexi points at the door. Shit, we forgot to lock it. I race over and lock the deadbolt. We finish getting dressed, throw a blanket over the evidence, and Lexi opens the door.

"Welcome home. How'd things go?"

Chapter Seventeen

Lexi

Before I can answer, Damien's cell rings, so he excuses himself and goes into the bedroom.

"Come sit out back and I'll fill you in. Do you want anything to drink?"

"Thanks, but I'm fine."

"It was tough on Damien and also on Jack's husband, Billy. I'm glad I could be there to help them. Even worse, Damien's father came to the service and the luncheon. Damien finally got a chance to get some closure, but it rattled him."

"I'm so happy you two found each other."

I watch a sad look sweep across my best friend's face.

"Are you okay?"

"Yeah. Just feeling sorry for myself. I know I always play like I'm happy being single, but I'm not. I see the way Damien looks at you. There's so much love and adoration in those gorgeous blue eyes. I want that."

"Perhaps from the coffee-colored eyes of a certain cowboy?"

"I mean, I wouldn't turn him down. But every time I think he might be interested, nothing."

"I wonder if someone hurt him. Maybe that's why he moved here from Texas."

"That would suck. He's such a sweet guy."

"He is. By the way, thanks for coming by to check on the dogs."

"Of course. I have to admit, I tried some of my best flirting on him, and no response." She sighs.

"I could have Damien talk to him. Not about you, but maybe he could find out some info about Judd's past. At least we would know what we're dealing with."

"I don't know."

"Well, I won't do anything if you don't want me to."

Damien comes outside after he finishes his phone call. A couple of minutes later, Judd appears at the fence. I see him look at Mel and there is definitely desire in those eyes. So why does he keep resisting her?

"Hey, Damien. Could I ask a favor?" Judd says.

"Sure, what's up?"

"I ran out of feed for my chickens. I'm a mess, so would you mind running to Tractor Supply and grabbing me a bag?"

"Of course."

"Thanks. They know what kind I use, so just let them know it's for me. I have an account there, so they can just put it on that."

"You got it. I'll be back."

Judd gives one more long look to Mel, then gets back to work. I look at her and she's practically got drool dripping down her chin.

"Do you need a napkin?"

"Shut up! Seriously, though, I need a girl's night."

"That sounds fun."

"I saw an ad that the club over in Lancaster is having ladies' night on Saturday. Wanna check it out?"

"Count me in!"

"Damien won't mind?" She asks me.

"Of course not. He's not like that. Besides, I was yours first!"

"And never forget it. I gotta run. I told them at work I'd be late. Wanted to check on you first."

"Thanks, girl. Love you."

"Love you too. I'll call before Saturday so we can decide what time."

"Looking forward to it."

While I wait for Damien to get home, I go out into the yard and play with the dogs some more. It's getting hot out, so I hook the sprinkler up to the hose so they can run through it. I see how much fun Maggie and Dave are having, so I figure what the hell. I join them and take my turn running through. Between the dogs barking and my laughter, I don't hear Damien get home until I feel myself leaving the ground.

Damien has me over his shoulder. He walks toward the pond, both dogs right behind him. Next thing I know, I'm in the pond. Damien and the dogs join me. Damien grabs me and pulls me close while the dogs splash around us. My clothes are stuck to me, but I don't care since I'm wrapped in Damien's sexy arms.

"Babe, I don't think I've wanted you more than I do right now."

"But I look like a mess."

"Oh no you don't. Your clothes clinging to your curves is, well, let's say I might have pitched a tent."

I stick my hand under the water, and sure enough, Damien is hard as a rock. I feel a heat building between my legs and all I want is to feel him inside me. I'm feeling especially naughty.

"Baby, fuck me right here in the pond."

"Damn, woman, are you sure? It's still light out."

"Fuck it. I don't give a damn if someone sees. I want you inside me so bad, I can't wait."

"You didn't get enough earlier?" He laughs.

"I could never get enough of my sexy Damien."

"Then get those shorts and panties off."

I get naked from the waist down.

"Now, get that ass over here."

I walk over to Damien. He picks me up and I wrap my legs around his waist. He bounces me up and down on his cock. Between feeling him inside me and the risk of getting caught, my body's on overdrive and I explode after only a few minutes. Damien puts me down.

"Babe, lay on the grass and spread those legs."

The feeling of the warm, soft grass on my naked ass feels so good.

Not as good as what I just felt, though. Damien lies on top of me, and I feel him slide inside me. His thrusts are slower and gentler this time. I love when he fucks me hard, but this side of him is just as exciting. I look into his eyes and smile as I wrap my arms around his neck.

"I love you, Lexi."

"Oh, Damien, I love you so much."

"This feels so good, babe."

"Mmm, but imagine if we were naked."

His jaw drops for a second, then he lifts my shirt off and removes his bra. I lift his shirt off. He holds me close as we make love under the warm summer sun. I feel his breathing speed up as he empties himself inside me. He lowers his head and kisses me with the same passion as the first time we ever kissed.

We're both drenched in sweat, so we get back in the pond to cool off. We splash, play and get so lost in each other that we don't hear a car pull into the driveway, until I look up and see Mel heading toward the pond.

"Shit. She's going to see our clothes."

"So what, babe? I think your best friend knows we fuck."

"Knowing it and catching us like this are two different things."

"You didn't care before."

"Because I was fucking horny."

Mel stops dead when she catches sight of our clothes laying on the ground. Her jaw drops, then she laughs at the top of her lungs. Just our luck. Judd is nearby and hears her, so he walks over to the fence. He sees our clothes and tries to hide a smile. Damien loves it, but I feel the heat spreading up my face.

Chapter Eighteen

Damien

I look over at Lexi, and her face is bright red. I try desperately not to laugh, but seeing Little Miss Naughty suddenly acting shy is funny. As if this moment needed any more humor, the dogs both jump in the pond. That's all it takes, and Lexi forgets about her embarrassment. She laughs as both dogs splash around her.

"Mel, could you get us each a towel so we can get out and dry off?" Lexi asks.

Mel is still laughing, so all she can do is nod yes. She walks into the house to get us towels.

"I'm gonna get back to work. I don't think I need to tell you two to have fun," Judd says.

He's about to leave when Mel comes back out. I see the look in his eyes and know that Lexi's right, but we still can't interfere. Without a word, he heads back to his farm. Mel hands us each a towel and turns around so we can get out of the pond and cover up.

"You can turn around now," Lexi says once we were wrapped in our towels.

"Who are you and what did you do with my friend? Seriously, though, this new version of you makes me beyond happy."

"Thanks! Damien gets most of the credit, though."

"I can see why," Mel says as she looks him up and down.

"Mel!"

"Hey, I am more than just eye candy, ya know!"

Lexi and Mel laugh and I put a fake pout on my face.

"Fine! I'm going to grab a shower and get dressed, so you two quit ogling me."

I head up to the shower and can hear the two of them laughing hysterically. I can only imagine what they're talking about. I wish my woman was in here with me. I love when those soft, sexy hands wash me. And watching the water stream down those sexy curves, fuck! As I'm showering, I run through Saturday in my mind to make sure I have everything covered.

Mel is going to treat Lexi to a spa day then clothes shopping to get ready for their "girls' night" at the club. While they're off getting pampered, Judd is going to help me set all the riddles up and get the dogs ready. He's hiding the ring, AKA "chicken feed" at his place. One of the best things about small-town life is having all the owners of the stops on the scavenger hunt agreeing to help. I'm just getting ready to rinse off when the bathroom door opens.

"I thought you might want some company."

"Get that sexy body in here, babe."

She drops her towel and steps in the shower with me. It doesn't matter how many times I see those sexy curves, my breath still catches in my throat. She grabs my shampoo and washes my hair. Her fingers on my scalp drive me crazy and my dick responds.

"Look what those fingers just did to me, babe."

"Oh my, Mr. Horndog. But you'll have to feed me first."

"Pizza?"

"Yes, please. Then, after dinner, I'll play with your salami."

"Fuck, woman."

We finish our showers and get dressed. We head down to Palermo's for pizza and beer, then stop at Dairy Queen for dessert. Lexi and I both order chocolate ice cream cones with chocolate jimmies. We sit down at one of the picnic tables to enjoy our treats. I watch Lexi twirling her tongue around the ice cream and I need to get her home now!

"Babe, hurry and finish. We NEED to get home."

She looks down at my crotch and smiles. We race home, take care of the dogs and spend the rest of the night in bed. Before I know it, Saturday is here and I'm a bundle of nerves. I'm grateful Mel is taking Lexi out early, so she won't get suspicious. Judd's primary assignment is to keep me calm. I can't think of anyone more equipped to handle the job.

We have a quick breakfast of cereal, which is good since I can barely stomach food. A little while later, Mel picks up Lexi. Mel texts me when they're inside the spa, so Judd and I get to work. We head to each of the stops on the scavenger hunt. Once everything is set up, we take the dogs to a groomer Mel found to get them ready. She bathes and dries each dog, then gets them dressed up. Dave is now sporting what looks like a tuxedo down his back, and Maggie has a small veil headpiece on. Now it's time to head back home and get ready myself.

Judd drops me off then heads home to get himself ready. After a quick shower, I get dressed. I'd forgotten what a quick shower felt like, as when Lexi's in there with me, we take a lot longer. I decide to go with my favorite navy blue dress pants. I pull on the perfectly tailored pants, add a cream colored short-sleeved shirt and dress shoes. I load the dogs in my car and head down to the dog park. I pulled some strings and got the park closed to the public today.

Judd pulls into the parking lot a few minutes after me. He's wearing black dress pants and a tan short-sleeved shirt, along with cowboy boots. I may have to keep Mel from passing out when she sees him. If all goes according to plan, it should be about an hour before Lexi and Mel arrive, giving me more than enough time to get nervous and change my speech a thousand times. Mel knows all the stops, so she can help push Lexi to answer the riddles if needed. About 45 minutes have passed when Judd's voice breaks the silence.

"Melissa just texted. They're on their way here."

I put my hand in my pocket to make sure the velvet box is still there. This is it, a moment I never thought I would experience. But this woman turned my life upside down in the best way possible. I knew from the first time I laid eyes on her, I would make her mine. As instructed, Mel has her blindfolded. She guides Lexi into the park and over to the spot where I'm standing. I nod, so Mel removes the blindfold. She walks over and stands next to Judd. He hands her Maggie's leash while he keeps hold of Dave's.

Lexi is an absolute vision. She's wearing a yellow sun dress, showing off her beautiful tan. Her hair is pulled back in a long ponytail with a fancy pearl clip. I see she's already tearing up as she looks at the dogs. I take a deep breath.

"Alexis Carter, you're unlike any woman I've ever known. You've taught me how amazing being in love is. From the moment I laid eyes on you, I wanted you. Since I've gotten to know you, I realized, for the first time in my life, what I truly wanted. Will you do me the honor of becoming my wife?"

Chapter Nineteen

Lexi

My jaw drops as I take in the scene in front of me. I smile when I see how the dogs are dressed. And holy shit, Damien looks hotter than hell. Did he really ask me what I think he did? I look at him, on one knee, holding a small box with a not-so-small diamond ring. Oh my lord, he did. And I'm standing here like an idiot, not saying anything.

"YES!"

Damien stands, takes the ring out of the box and slips it on my finger. The waterworks come full force as he pulls me close and kisses me tenderly. Judd and Melissa circle around us, and the four of us stand here in a group hug. We all separate when we hear the dogs barking. I laugh at how overdressed we are all for the dog park.

"We have dinner reservations at The Log Cabin in Leola. We just need to drop the dogs off," Damien says.

"Melissa, you're welcome to ride with me," Judd says.

"Thank you," Melissa says.

I ride home with Damien and the dogs. Melissa and Judd follow us.

Damien takes the dogs inside while Mel gets into Judd's truck. They follow us to the restaurant. When we arrive, the maitre d takes us to The Gable Room, one of the restaurant's private rooms. I'm normally a pizza place or diner girl, but this is a nice change.

Damien orders a bottle of champagne. He pours us each a glass. We all drink a toast to Damien's and my engagement. I order the mocha rubbed ribeye steak with a side of truffle fries for dinner and the chocolate peanut butter bomb for dessert. The food is heavenly, so I ignore how many calories I consumed.

"I don't even want to know how many calories were in my dessert," I say.

"Don't worry, babe. I have a feeling we'll work it off later."

And just like that, my panties are soaked. Mel and Judd snicker. Damien flashes me a look that just about melted my panties right off. After we finish dinner and polish off the rest of the champagne, we head home. Judd drops Mel at our house so she can get her car. After they both head home, we feed the dogs and take them outside. Once they do their business and play a little, we go back inside.

Damien turns on some music and pulls me into his arms. His hands slide under my dress and plant themselves on my ass. Wait until he sees the see-through lace bra and panties under my dress. The thought of someone looking at me used to terrify me. Since I met Damien, it excites me more than I ever thought was possible. I unbutton his shirt and gawk at his sexy, chiseled chest. I picture running my tongue all over him. He unzips my dress and lets it fall to the floor. His jaw drops as he looks at me and I get even wetter. I'm standing there in a sheer, white bra and panties set. Damien can't speak and his feet are firmly planted on the floor.

"See something you like?"

"Holy fuckin' shit, woman! I want you so fuckin' bad, I can't stand it."

"Oh, Damien. Please take me to bed."

He scoops me up in his arms. I wrap my arms around his neck and lay my head on his shoulder. He carries me to the bedroom and lays me down on the bed. I watch him remove his clothes. My eyes scan him from head to toe. Damn, he's the sexiest man I've ever seen. Part of me still can't believe he's mine, but then I look at my finger. His dick is already hard as he walks over to the bed.

I lift my hips off the bed so he can slide my panties off. My bra is a front-closure, so he easily opens and removes it. He wraps me in his arms and kisses me tenderly. We lie there kissing for a deliciously long time. I love the change in things tonight.

"Babe, I've never been as happy as I was when I heard you say yes."

"I'm so happy. I couldn't have asked for a better proposal. I love the way you dressed up the dogs. But right now, I want to focus on this moment. I need to feel you make love to me tonight."

Damien takes a hand and runs his fingers lightly between my breasts, sending chills through my entire body. He slowly drags his fingers down my belly until he reaches my pussy. Instead of touching me where I want him most, he runs his hand down one leg and up the other. My breathing shallows as I feel an aching throb between my legs.

"Please, Damien. Please, touch me now."

He lies down next to me and pulls my body toward his, lifting me slightly off the bed. His hand caresses my ass as we kiss. He's driving me wild and I love it. I never want this moment to end, so I love that he's taking things slow. I try to push him onto his back, but he stops me.

"No, no, no. You wanted me to make love to you tonight, so I'm in charge."

"Oh, Damien. I want you so much."

As he kisses me, he traces the outside of my ear with a finger. He moves his lips to my neck and sucks lightly. He runs his tongue along my throat. He moves to the other side of my neck and sucks again. I'm dripping between my legs, my desire for him reaching the boiling point. Still, he takes things slow.

His mouth continues its journey, stopping at each of my breasts. He sucks them one at a time, lightly nibbling on each nipple. The sweet sting of his teeth has me moaning and writhing on the bed. I reach my hands out and touch him everywhere I can reach. He has himself positioned, though, so I can't reach his cock. I settle for his ass and give it a big squeeze.

"Behave yourself, woman, or I'll make you wait longer."

He runs his tongue down to my belly, then showers me with light kisses, followed by some gentle bites. If he doesn't touch my pussy soon, I'm going to spontaneously combust. Still, he tortures and moves down to my legs. He sucks the inside of both of my thighs. He's so close to the promised land I can't stand it. He trails his tongue down my left leg and kisses the top of my foot. After repeating the same with my right leg, he works his way back up my body, still refusing to give me what I want most.

"Damien, I can't take much more of this. I'm aching for your touch."

"I've been touching you."

"But not there."

"Where?"

"You know where!"

"I don't think I do. Tell me, babe. Where do you want me to touch you? And you better make me want to!"

Chapter Twenty

Damien

I'm watching her. Watching the way she's writhing on the bed. I know exactly where she wants me to touch her. But it gets me even hotter when I hear her tell me. I think back to the first time I saw her at the club. She was so shy, she couldn't even watch me on the stage. Now, this woman can't get enough of me. Of having sex with me. Of being fucked by me. The dirty way she talks in bed is incredible. I love hearing her sultry, low voice uttering the filthiest of words. I despise women with high-pitched voices. Not my Lexi. Her voice is so fucking sexy.

"Oh Damien. I need to feel you touching my pussy. I'm so fucking wet for you. I crave your tongue licking me, your lips sucking me. Please, baby."

"What else do you want, woman?"

"I want your fingers inside me. I want to feel you stroking my clit."

I feign a yawn.

"That's it, babe? I'm still not convinced."

"I want your cock as deep inside me as it will go. Please, Damien, please fuck me, baby."

"We've done all that before. I think I'll just go get dressed now."

Then, somehow, this sexy woman shocks me.

"Babe, please spank my pussy."

Holy. Fucking. Shit. Did I just hear that correctly? My mouth opens wide, but no words come out. I didn't know it was possible, but my dick gets even harder. She wants me to do what. Holy shitballs. I've always wanted to do that to her. Not to hurt her, but to please her. I feared how she would react, so I never mentioned it.

"I'm sorry. I went too far," I hear a quiet voice say.

"No, babe, you didn't. I'm just speechless. I've wanted to do that for so long, but I was too nervous at how you'd respond."

"Please, Damien. I want to feel that so fucking bad."

I watch her spread her legs wide. Those beautiful hands of hers spread her pussy wide and I almost shoot my load right on the spot. I lightly swat her pussy, glistening with desire. I follow it with a couple more light swats as she moans.

"Mmmm, Damien. More. Please."

But I want to tease her, so I stop. I don't touch her at all, and I stand up. I watch her lying there, writhing. I can see how badly she wants, and I want her just as bad. But I also want her to feel things she's never felt, and the longer I tease her, the longer she has to expect what's coming, the more pleasure she'll experience. Time to take things up a notch.

"Close those beautiful green eyes, babe."

I walk over to our dirty drawer, grab a few things, and return to the bed.

"Open your eyes."

She looks at what I'm holding and a smile spreads across her face. Damn this woman. She takes the blindfold and puts it on herself.

"Eager, aren't we, Lexi?"

"I. WANT. YOU. SO. FUCKING. BAD."

"Fuck, babe!"

I take the two black scarves I'm holding and tie each of her wrists to the headboard. I love seeing her like this. The smile still hasn't left her beautiful face. I grab one vibrator and turn it on high. I touch it to her clit and her body bucks off the bed. I hold it against her clit as she writhes and moans loudly.

"So fucking good, Damien."

I turn it off and just watch her again. It's impossible to take my eyes off this naked beauty. I don't know how much more I can stand. My cock is screaming at me to get inside her. I talk him off the ledge for now and turn my focus back to pleasuring her. This amazing woman who taught me how to love again, who today agreed to become my wife, deserves nothing less than the best. That includes how I treat her in bed. But enough teasing. It's time to turn the heat up higher than ever.

"Where are you, my sexy Damien? I want you."

"I hope you're ready for this, babe!"

"Mmmm, yes, please."

"Good girl."

I climb on top of her and lower my mouth around one of her delectable tits. I suck her nipple hard, nipping it, while I tease her other nipple with my fingers until they're both almost as hard as my dick. I skip her stomach this time, as all I want now is to taste that sweet pussy. I slide down her soft body until my head's between her silky thighs.

"Open those legs as wide as you can, babe."

She spreads her legs again, and all I can do is stare at that hot pussy. So wet. So inviting. I take my tongue and swipe up slowly. I flick her clit a couple of times with my tongue. She writhes against my face. I give her clit a quick nip with my teeth, then suck her hard. I feel her getting close, so I stop.

"No, please, don't stop."

"Show me how you want to be touched, babe."

I grab my dick and stroke as I watch her slide a couple of fingers inside her own pussy. She moans as she slides them in and out. Fuck! I grab her hand and suck her fingers, enjoying the taste of her. I cover her pussy with my mouth, alternating between swiping with my tongue and sucking her clit hard.

"Oh fuck, I'm so close. Please spank my pussy until I come for you."

"Goddamn, woman. You're so fucking hot."

I spank her pussy and stroke her clit hard with my fingers. I feel her body quaking. I stop for a minute to remove her blindfold.

"I want you to watch me finish you."

"Mmmm. Make me squirt."

I slide my fingers inside her and stroke her g-spot hard while I suck her clit. Her body bucks as I feel her soak my face. She tastes so fucking sweet. I untie her wrists so she doesn't hurt herself. I suck her clit as she comes over and over. Her hands are gripping the bed as she screams at the top of her lungs.

"OH. FUCK. Oh, Damien. So good. Mmmm. Please, god, get that cock inside me now."

I lie on my back next to her and wag my finger at her. She peels herself off the bed and climbs on top of me. I feel her soaking wet pussy slide down the full length of my dick. She sits up straight, giving me a full view of those sexy double-Ds. I grab her sexy ass while she rides me. Her pace is slow, sliding up and down my dick until I'm ready to explode. She stops moving and just sits there with my dick inside her.

"Babe, what are you trying to do to me?"

"Make it last, sexy."

I try to thrust into her.

"Oh no you don't. Keep that up and I'll climb off."

"No, please. I love feeling you wrapped around my dick."

She climbs off anyway and gets on all fours. Her lips wrap around my balls and she sucks lightly. She moves her pretty mouth to my dick and takes my entire length down her throat. I'm still impressed at how she can handle me. My fingers stroke her clit as she sucks me until I come down her throat. She collapses next to me, both of us drenched in sweat and god knows what else.

"Holy fucking hell, woman."

"Oh my god, Damien, that was incredible."

That was the last thing I remembered until the next morning.

Chapter Twenty-One

Lexi

"Get that cute little ass out of bed."

I stretch as I wake up. When I open my eyes, I see Damien and the dogs staring at me. Damien has one suitcase packed and another sitting there empty. Did I miss something? How long was I asleep after that major pussy-pounding? I smile, remembering how much fun we had in bed yesterday.

"What's going on? Did you rob a bank?"

"Huh?"

"I thought we had to make a quick getaway."

"Funny, babe. Now get your ass moving."

"Where are we going?" I ask.

"We got sidetracked and never took that trip to Maine."

"Oh my god, we're going! But what about the two wiggle-butts?"

"I may have bought a camper, so they're coming with us."

"Oh yay. I just need to grab a quick shower and get packed."

"Move it, or we leave without you, woman!"

"Okay, okay, dickhead. I'm going."

I zip through a shower, skip the blow dryer, and throw on denim shorts and a t-shirt. Damien takes one look at me, and his jaw drops. Time to have a little fun. I bend over in front of him and give my ass a little shake. I hear him groan.

"Woman, you're going to pay for that!"

"You promise?"

That earns me a swat on the ass. I get my clothes and toiletries packed, then head downstairs to help Damien get the dogs' stuff packed. Once we're done, we load up his car and get on the road. We hit Dunkin' Donuts drive-through for breakfast since the dogs are with us. We get back on the road and drive until we hit an RV park in Massachusetts. It's nearing dusk, so we camp here for the night. We get up early the next morning and drive the rest of the way to Bar Harbor, Maine.

Damien drives us to Seawall Campgrounds in Acadia National Park. He rented an RV space for us. Once we get settled, we head into town and grab some food. We have a small fridge, so we grab milk and a few other essentials, like cereal and some snacks. We get back to the trailer and secure all the food in the cabinets.

"Do you want anything to eat?" I ask.

"I do."

"What do you want?"

"You out of your pants."

"Then I think I know what you want to eat."

"Mmmm, yes, my delicious woman."

"There'll be plenty of time for that later. I thought we could take the dogs for a walk since we've had them cooped up in the truck for so long."

"Fine, but I will get you naked later."

"We'll see."

"Yes we will, woman!"

I laugh as we get the dogs ready for the walk. Damien takes Dave's leash and I hold Maggie's. Damien takes my free hand in his, and my insides melt. I've never felt love for anyone before. And unlike those asshats in my past, he treats me the way I deserve to be treated. I wish I had figured that out sooner. I could have spared myself a lot of pain, but it makes me appreciate this sexy man even more.

After walking for about an hour, we stop to let the dogs rest and have some water. We take a seat in the grass and Damien puts his arm around me. I look over and our eyes meet. All these months later and I still melt like ice cream on a hot summer day. He leans in and kisses me tenderly, gently sliding his tongue into my mouth. If there weren't other people around, I'd already be naked. This man excites me more than I ever knew was possible.

I give the dogs one more drink of water, then we continue our walk. The campground is a quiet wooded area with a nice walking trail. We're also within walking distance of the coastline and only 18 miles away from Bar Harbor. We head back to our camper, stopping one more time to rest the dogs and give them water then finish our walk. As soon as we're inside the camper, the dogs curl up and fall asleep. Damien leads me over to the bed.

"Babe, please come to bed with me. I want you so damn much."

"Oh, Damien. Strip, lie down and don't take those sexy eyes off me."

I grab my phone and scroll through my favorite music app. When I find what I'm looking for, I press play. The sexy vocals of Keith St. John come out of my phone as I treat Damien to a striptease to 'Sex Machine' by Burning Rain. The more I move for him, the more I see his dick grow. I put my finger in my mouth and run it down my body, stopping between my legs. I give myself a quick tease and Damien's jaw drops. He grabs his dick.

"Babe, I need you here. Now!"

"Is that right? I'm not convinced you really want me."

"Babe, look at my dick."

"Sorry, but you'll have to convince me to ride that thing!"

"Woman, I want nothing more than to feel your hot, wet pussy wrapped around me. I love watching those sexy tits bounce when you take every inch of me deep inside that gorgeous body. Please, babe."

I climb onto the bed and lick the pre-cum off his rock hard erection. Fuck, he tastes incredible, but not as incredible as how he feels. I straddle him, slowly lowering myself down. I savor each inch as I take him all the way inside my body. I moan as he touches every sensitive spot inside me. I angle my body so my clit rubs his dick as I rock my hips.

"Fuck, you feel so damn good inside my pussy. But I've also been a naughty girl. Please spank me while I fuck you."

I sound like a tigress when his hand connects with my ass. Fuck, the sweet sting of being spanked while his dick is setting my pussy on fire is like nothing I've ever felt. I ride him harder. I'm getting close to exploding and I can't take it. I climb off, lay on my back and spread my legs.

"Please, baby, make me come with that hot tongue."

I watch as Damien puts his head between my thighs. I come undone when I feel his tongue on my clit. My whole body bucks off the bed as I scream. If there's anyone else nearby, they are getting quite the audible treat right now. A steady stream of very dirty words escapes my lips. Damien smiles as he slides up my body. He thrusts into me fast and hard, pounding me until I feel him empty inside me. Not having enough energy to even get dressed, we pull up the covers and sleep until the following morning.

Chapter Twenty-Two

Damien

I wake up alone the following morning. My woman's taste is still on my tongue and damn, it's incredible. I walk outside and see Lexi sitting in the grass with the dogs, so I join them. I love our awesome but unconventional family. I hate that anyone thought Lexi was damaged goods because she couldn't have children. She has so much more than that to offer this world.

"Good morning, beautiful," I say after I sit.

"Mmm, it sure was a good night, baby."

"Fuck yeah. I can still taste that sweet pussy."

"How about I replace that with some coffee and breakfast?"

"I like your taste best, but I am kinda hungry, so that sounds good."

I watch my sexy fiancee get up and head inside the camper. I still can't believe I'm lucky enough to get to love her for the rest of my days. She's my everything and I will protect her at all costs. A little while later, she opens the camper door and the dogs perk up. I'm greeted with the smell of bacon. No wonder the dogs are drooling. I get up and take them inside. Lexi has two plates made up of scrambled eggs, bacon, and an English muffin. There's also two cups of coffee on the little dining table. I see a small plate with a couple of extra pieces of bacon for the dogs.

"I thought we could unhook the camper and take the dogs for a ride today," I say to Lexi after breakfast.

Maggie and Dave hear the word ride and start barking like crazy. Lexi laughs, another sound I will never tire of hearing.

"I'd love to. I've never been here, so I would love a tour."

"Great. Let me clean up, then we can go."

"I'll clean up."

"No way, babe. You cooked, so I'm cleaning."

"Who am I to argue?"

After I'm done cleaning up, we pack up some water and treats for the dogs, along with some snacks for us. I take Lexi through the rest of Acadia park. I'd forgotten how beautiful the park was. I look over at my woman, and the smile won't come off her face. I love how she always appreciates the beauty of things, though everything pales compared to her stunning beauty.

I take her to some other sites around the town as she furiously snaps pictures. I love that she still uses a regular camera instead of her cell phone like everyone else. She also prints all her pictures and puts them into albums, which I find refreshing. I think about how I'd love to have an album of naked pictures of her. Shit, there goes my dick stirring again. I talk myself down for now, though I plan on playing with her later. By the time we finish the tour, it's nearing dinnertime and I'm getting hungry.

"How about we grab some takeout and head back to the campground, babe?"

"Sounds good. Could we get some pizza?"

"Exactly what I was thinking."

We head down to a local pizza place. I run in while Lexi waits with the dogs. We head back and sit outside, enjoying the cool New England summer evening. After we eat, we feed the dogs, then take them for a walk around the campground. Once the sun is almost down, we go back inside the camper and watch one of the movies I downloaded onto my tablet since there was no wi-fi here.

The rest of the week flies by and before we know it, it's time to start the journey back home. We get an earlier start, so we do the entire drive back to Pennsylvania in one day. We're all exhausted, so we have a quick bite to eat and hang out on the couch until we decide to head to bed. Unpacking can wait until tomorrow.

After sleeping until mid-morning, we're in the kitchen enjoying brunch when I hear a knock at the door. I open the door to Melissa standing there, her eyes puffy and her nose red. I walk her to the kitchen and pour her a cup of coffee. She sits down across from Lexi and grabs her hand. I lean against the counter while they chat.

"Oh my god, Mel, what's wrong?" Lexi asks her best friend.

"There was an accident while you were gone."

"What? Who?"

"Doug and Meg. They were crossing Main when a driver ran the red light."

"Did they? I mean, how are they?"

"Sweetie, they didn't make it."

I feel helpless as Lexi gasps. I walk over and crouch between them, hugging them both as they sob. Doug was one of the few people who didn't treat Lexi like shit when they were in school together. Why do the good ones always seem to get taken so early? First Jack, now Doug and Meg. I look at my Lexi and all I want is to take that pain away from her. I hate when she's hurting. Mel stands up after she finishes her coffee. Lexi stands up and gives her a big hug.

"The services are this Friday. Would you mind if I came here and rode with you two?"

I see Lexi look at me. "Of course, no problem," I say.

"Call me if you need to talk," Mel says as she walks toward the door.

"I will. Love you, Mel," Lexi says, holding Mel's hand and walking with her.

"Love you, girl."

After Mel's gone, I walk Lexi over to the couch and we sit down. I wrap my arms around her and feel her head on my shoulder. She's shaking and I can feel tears on my arm. I stand and scoop her off the couch. I carry her to bed and I hold her until she finally falls asleep. A couple of hours pass and I feel her stir. I hear her stomach rumble.

"How about some dinner, babe?"

She nods and whispers that she wants Chinese, so I call in a delivery order. We walk to the living room and wait for the food. After dinner, we take the dogs for a walk. The walk also takes Lexi's mind off what happened for a little while. We get back home and spend a quiet night together, just watching some TV. Around 11, Lexi lets out an enormous yawn. We take the dogs out for their last bathroom break and head off to bed.

We're awakened the following morning by Lexi's cell phone. She answers and listens to whoever's on the other end. I watch her face change expressions a few times and I wonder what's going on. She finishes the call with her mouth hanging open. When she finally disconnects, I look at her, curious about what that was all about.

"Babe, you look stunned. What's going on?"

Chapter Twenty-Three

Lexi

"That was the attorney for the club."

"Why were they calling you?" Damien asks me.

"Doug left the club to me."

"Excuse me, what did you just say?"

"You heard me right. He had explicit instructions that if anything ever happened to him and Meg together, that ownership was to be transferred to me. It further states that I should use it to follow my dream of having a bookstore."

"What are you going to do, babe?"

"I don't know. I know this is my dream, but the circumstances." I sigh.

"Babe, I know losing your friend is awful, but you owe it to him to honor his wishes."

"You're right, but I'm also not going to turn it into just a bookstore. I'm going to keep at least the bar part and his staff."

"Another of my favorite things about you."

"What?"

"You always think of others first."

"That hasn't always served me well, but this is different."

"I get it and I love you for it. What do you need to do now?"

"I'm meeting with the club's lawyer in the morning to sign the papers. Will you come with me?" I ask him.

"Of course. Do you think you should also bring an attorney?"

"I don't have one. Where would I find someone on short notice?"

"Dean's friend Chris is the DA. He could recommend someone."

"You don't think he'd mind?"

"No. I'll give him a buzz now."

"Thanks."

While Damien calls Dean, I take the dogs outside to play. I see Judd is hard at work, as always. I really hope somehow he and Mel find their way to each other, but I need to just let it happen. I love my friend and I want to see her happy. I sometimes get a feeling there's something she's not telling me. Judd is also a bit of a mystery. Maybe someday, we'll learn his story too. My thoughts get interrupted by the sexiest voice I've ever heard.

"Dean gave me a name. Chris is going to let her know you'll be calling and she'll go with you."

"Thanks, baby. Now, how about some breakfast?"

I watch my future husband walk over. He pulls me in close and plants a kiss on me that threatens to boil my blood.

"I know what I want to eat."

"Damien!"

"What?"

"Is that all you think about?"

"Oh, and you don't. You know you love this," he says, pointing at his crotch.

I put my hands on his ass and jam my tongue in his mouth.

"I do, but I'm starving."

"Babe, that was mean!"

"I'll make up for it later, sexy."

"Damn right you will. But for now, how about we let someone else cook for a change?"

"Sounds good."

After giving the furries their breakfast, we head out to our favorite diner. I'm still a bit in shock about the phone call I got this morning. Not to mention the reason for the call. I still can't believe my friend is gone. It's why I'm determined to honor his wishes.

"Can we ride by the club after breakfast?"

"Sure, babe. Why?"

"I'm not sure. It just feels like I need to do it. I don't want to go in or do anything. I just feel like I need to see it."

"You got it, babe."

After we eat. Damien takes care of the check and tip while I walk outside. I can't help feeling unsettled. I've dealt with a lot since we got home from our trip. The self-doubt kicks in. Am I going to handle owning a business? Will I succeed? Will people still come if I change it? That a bunch of other questions fill my head and by the time Damien comes outside, I'm a hot mess.

As if he can read my mind, Damien grabs my hand and says, "Babe, it's all going to be fine. You're not in this alone."

I smile and say, "I'm scared."

"I get it."

We walk to his car and drive over to the club. The club's closed, so we park right in front of the doors. There's a note stating the club is closed until further notice. In front of the doors are bouquets of flowers and small stuffed animals. It warms my heart that so many people knew what a great man Doug was. I hear my phone alert me that a new text came in.

"Mel just sent me a link to the obituary."

Damien hugs me as we stand there staring at the memorial. Neither of us says a word. After a few more minutes, we head back to the car and drive home. My cell rings on the way home. I don't recognize the number, but something tells me to answer this one, anyway.

"Hello."

"Hello. May I please speak to Lexi?" a polite older woman says. I know the voice right away,

"I'm so sorry, Mrs. Matthews."

"Thanks, sweetie. I'm calling to see if you'd be willing to sing at the funeral. My Dougie always talked about how talented you are."

"It's my honor. Is there a particular song, so I make sure I learn it?"

"Yes. Doug had it in his last wishes for you to sing Stairway to Heaven. He said it had special meaning for the two of you."

"It does." I smile, knowing I can never tell her why.

"Thank you, honey. We'll see you on Friday."

"I really am sorry."

I disconnect the call. I glance over and see Damien looking at me like he wants to ask me something.

"I know what you want to ask, and it's fine."

"Babe, only if you're comfortable."

I walk over and sit down on the couch. He may regret asking me. I've told no one this, even Mel. Damien sits down next to me and puts his arm around me. I'm not sure I want him sitting here like this with what I'm about to tell him.

"Are you sure you want to hear this?"

"Babe, you're making me nervous now."

"It's just, I haven't talked much about certain things with you. But, well, it happened a long time ago."

"What happened?"

"I know. I've already told you how the other kids treated me. What I didn't tell you is that it also included nobody wanting to date me. I didn't have a single date in four years of high school. I went to the prom, but Doug and I went as friends. Then summer came, and we were both preparing for our first year in college."

I hesitate for a moment. Should I be telling Damien this? Is he going to be mad? My head is spinning. I look at Damien and he's smiling. Does he know already? How could he know? I never even told Mel. I'm freaking out. Shit. I take a deep breath and continue.

"We were in his room hanging out and talking about both of us going to college as 18-year-old loser virgins. Something neither of us wanted. So, we talked about it some more and, well, let's just say neither of us went to college as a virgin."

I feel the heat spreading up my cheeks as I watch for Damien's reaction. He's looking at me all stone-faced. Shit. I knew I shouldn't have told him. I just messed up the best thing I've ever had. Why can't I ever keep my damn mouth shut? Tears fill my eyes. I try to wipe them away, but they spill over.

"Babe, what's wrong?" He asks me.

"I'm so sorry."

"For what?"

"Messing up our relationship."

"What?"

"I knew I shouldn't have told you."

"Babe, I'm not mad."

"But the look on your face."

"Truthfully, I was trying not to laugh." He smiles at me.

"What?"

"Babe, I thought it was cute how freaked out you were. I could never get mad at you about something that happened that long ago. I'm curious though, what does that have to do with Stairway?"

"Get ready to laugh again. That song came on right as we were, um, starting. And let's just say we finished before the song. In fairness, though, we were horny teenagers who'd never done it before."

Suddenly, I can't control my laughter. Damien joins me, both of us just sitting there in hysterics. As quickly as the laughter came, my mood changes. I feel angry.

"It's so fucking unfair that he's gone."

"I know it seems that way, but there's no way we can know what the future has in store."

"But why someone so good as Doug?"

"I asked myself that same question about Jack. We can't change what happened to them, but we can control how we move forward. Jack would want me to keep living. It's obvious Doug wanted the same for you. Otherwise, he wouldn't have left his club to you. If it hadn't been for those two men, we wouldn't be here together at this moment."

"I love you."

"I love you, babe."

Damien grabs another pillow and puts it on his lap. He gently pulls me down so my head's resting on the pillow. He rubs my back as a fresh round of tears slide down my face. I wake up a couple of hours later when I feel Damien shift.

"Stay here, babe. I'll heat some leftovers for dinner."

"Thanks."

Once he's done, we take leftover Chinese food outside so the dogs can play while we eat. We spend a quiet evening in bed watching TV, the dogs curled up at our feet. The last thing I remember was Phoebe singing Smelly Cat at Central Perk. I awaken in the morning to Damien gently shaking me, so I can get ready for my appointment.

Chapter Twenty-Four

Damien

Lexi's appointment went very well. I watched her, unable to stop smiling as her dreams came true. The circumstances weren't what anyone wanted, but she's determined to honor Doug's legacy. He'd done well for himself and left her plenty of money to handle things.

First, though, I need to help her get through the funeral, the way she helped me with Jack's. I get up early and let her sleep. I grab the griddle and make French toast. When breakfast is done, I gently wake her.

"Sweetie, breakfast is ready."

"I'm not hungry."

"You need to eat. I know today is going to be hard. It's my turn to take care of you."

I put my hand out, and she takes it. I keep her hand in mine and walk her to the table. I bring her a cup of coffee and a plate of French toast. She looks at me, her eyes filling with tears.

"I can't do this."

"I felt that way when Jack passed, but babe, you can. You're so much stronger than you let yourself believe. You need to sing today, and I'm going to be there supporting you. And it turns out, I'm not the only one. Dean texted earlier. He and Alex are coming. Judd's also coming to support you and Mel."

"Thanks, Damien. Can I ask a favor?"

"Anything, babe."

"Will you play the guitar for me?"

"You got it."

I kiss the top of her head and sit down to join her for breakfast. After we eat, we shower and get dressed. We're both wearing the same outfits we wore to Jack's services. This one isn't any easier. Even though I don't have the same personal loss as last time, Lexi does, and my heart breaks for her. I just hope that what we do at the club will help her cope.

Judd walks over and we head out to pick up Mel on the way to the funeral home. Judd gets up front with me while the girls ride in the backseat together. I can see both of them crying. I hope Lexi can get through the song, but if she can't, I'll take over. I'm glad I'm going to be up there accompanying her.

We pull into the parking lot a little early, but we get out and wait at the doors. The funeral director eyes my guitar.

"My girlfriend is singing at the service. I'll be playing for her."

"Are you Lexi?"

"Yes, sir."

"Mr. and Mrs. Matthews asked me to send you and Damien in when you arrived. Follow me, please."

I turn to look at Judd, who nods. He puts an arm around Mel to comfort her until they can join us when the viewing officially starts. I take Lexi's hand as we prepare to walk into the room. She looks at the double casket and her knees buckle. I put the guitar case down and hold on to her. We walk over to Doug's and Meg's parents. Lexi hugs each of them while I keep a hand on her for support. I shake everyone's hands. Doug's dad shows me where to set up my guitar.

The doors have now opened and mourners are filing in. Judd and Mel make their way through the line, then join Lexi and me. I watch the door intently, watching for Bryan and Amy. I hope they have the decency not to attend. That's the last thing Lexi needs to deal with. Dean and Alex arrive and join us.

We take seats off to the side so we don't have to make anyone move when it's Lexi's time to sing. We get to the end of the visitation portion and I'm relieved that I haven't seen Amy and Bryan. Once the last few mourners make their way to seats, the pastor walks up front and begins the service. Lexi told me he was the same pastor who performed Doug and Meg's wedding. He speaks for a few moments, then calls Lexi up to sing.

I walk her up to the stools that were set up for us. Once she's seated, I grab my guitar and start playing. I watch her take a deep breath and open her mouth. No words come out at first, so I play the intro again. This time, she sings, and she sounds like an angel. Looking around at the mourners, you could see the effect her voice had on everyone. Even though Judd had tears in his eyes. Her voice cracked about halfway through and she couldn't recover.

Dean and Alex came up to the front. Alex took Lexi to sit while Dean finished the song for her. Alex held Lexi close while she sobbed. Dean and I finished the song and took the seats Lexi and I had been using. Once the service was over, Dean and I walked over to our women.

"Thank you, Dean. I'm so embarrassed that I couldn't finish."

"Don't be. I wouldn't have been able to get even that far had it been Chris," Dean said.

"Thank you to you too, Alex."

"Any time. Call me if you ever want to talk."

"Thank you."

Dean and Alex headed out while the rest of us walked to the parking lot. Once they loaded the casket into the hearse, the procession to the cemetery started. Lexi said little on the ride there. Once we arrived, we parked where they directed us. The four of us walked over to the tent and waited for the interment to begin. After a brief service, we laid our flowers on the casket. We walked back to our cars and drove to the restaurant where the luncheon was being held. We walked inside and took a table in the corner.

"How're you holdin' up, babe?"

"I don't wanna do any more of these."

"I know, sweetie. Me either."

Once everyone arrived, both families said a few words, followed by the pastor. They called one table at a time to get their food. Judd and I went up together to get lunch for us and Mel and Lexi. After we finished eating, Lexi and Mel said goodbye to Doug's and Meg's parents, then we headed home. We dropped Mel off, then Judd. When we got home, Lexi sat down on the couch.

"Babe, how about a nice soak in the tub, then a quiet evening in our jammies?"

"That sounds perfect."

We go upstairs and while Lexi's getting undressed, I put a lavender-scented bath bomb in the tub and turn the water on. Once the tub is full, I help Lexi in, then get undressed and join her. I turn on the jets and we both lean back and relax. After we're done, I help Lexi out, then get out and drain the tub. We dry off and walk to the bedroom to get in our pajamas.

We head back downstairs. Lexi gets Maggie and Dave their dinner while I microwave a bag of popcorn. We decide on reruns of The Office. Once we've taken the dogs out to use the bathroom, I open the sofa-bed. We settle in and spend the next several hours laughing at the crazy antics of Michael, Dwight, Jim and the rest of the crew. Just once, I want to put something of someone's in Jello!

Lexi eventually falls asleep. I don't have the heart to wake her, so I put the dogs out for one last potty break. I lock up and turn the TV and lights off. I get back on the sofa-bed, cover us with a blanket. I snuggle up to her, the last thing I recall until morning.

We're sitting out back enjoying breakfast when Judd comes to the fence.

"Hey, man, come join us?"

"I can't. I just wanted to tell you I'm going away for a while. Could I ask a favor?"

"Of course."

"Could you take care of my animals while I'm gone?"

"You got it. Everything okay?" I ask.

"I hope so. I'm leaving in an hour. Here's all the instructions, including where to buy more food. I have an account, so you won't have to put out any money. I'm not sure how long I'll be gone. Are you sure this is okay?"

"We are. Take care and I hope everything works out."

"I second what Damien said. Call if you need anything."

"Thank you both."

Before I can respond, he's gone. I look at Lexi.

"What the hell, babe?"

"Your guess is as good as mine."

We spend the rest of the summer getting the club ready for a Labor Day re-opening and taking care of Judd's farm. We also start talking about wedding plans. We're looking at a couple potential dates, though I know which way I'm leaning...

The End... for now!

About the Author

Samantha Michaels was born in 1973 in the small town of Abington, PA and was raised and still lives in Hatboro, PA (both suburbs of Philadelphia). She is married to her high school sweetheart and they have a rescue dog, a beautiful Black Lab named Holly.

When she's'not writing or working at her full-time job, she enjoys watching her Philly sports team (hopefully) win, listening to heavy metal/hard rock music, Texas Hold Em, reading, and spending time with friends and family.

Her love of reading began at a young age, thanks to her mother and Sesame Street. Her mom read to her constantly, and by three years old, she was reading on her own, and hasn't stopped. This eventually turned into a love of writing. She was writing for herself and then for a small group of friends, one of whom told her she should be writing books. She took her friends advice and has since published several romance books with plenty more on the way.

For updates and a free book, click **here** to sign up for my newsletter.

Also by
Samantha Michaels

The Rockstar Quadrilogy

Leather and Lace

A Second Shot at Love

Pet Shop Passion

Silent Angel - Coming April 2022

The Melody of the Seasons

Rockin' Spring

Rockin' Summer

Rockin' Autumn - Coming September 2022

Rockin' Winter - Coming December 2022

www.ingramcontent.com/pod-product-compliance
Lightning Source LLC
Chambersburg PA
CBHW020153180626
46810CB00004B/1870